Benjamin Lebert
Crazy

Benjamin Lebert was born in Freiburg in 1982. He writes articles for the young-adult supplement of the *Süddeutsche Zeitung*, Munich's leading newspaper. He lives in Berlin.

VINTAGE

INTERNATIONAL

Crazy

Crazy

Benjamin Lebert

Translated from the German by
Carol Brown Janeway

Vintage International

Vintage Books
A Division of Random House, Inc.
New York

For Bruno Schnee and Norbert Lebert

We are all potentially characters in a novel—with the difference that characters in a novel really get to live their lives to the full.

—GEORGES SIMENON

Crazy

Chapter 1

So this is where I'm supposed to stay. Until I graduate, if possible. That's the plan. I stand in the parking lot of Castle Neuseelen Boarding School and look around. My parents are standing beside me. They brought me here. I've got four schools behind me now. This is to be my fifth. And the fifth is finally supposed to raise my damn math score from a 6 to a 5. I can't wait.

They've already been sending letters and encouraging messages along the lines of: *Dear Benjamin, Just come to us and everything will get better. Lots of people before you have made it already.*

Of course they have. There are always enough pupils for one or more of them to make it. I know that already. But things are a bit different with me. I'm sixteen and I'm repeating ninth grade. The way it looks, I'm not going to make it this time either. My parents are both respected people—doctor of alternative medicine and engineer. They can't be seen to be giving some mere middle-school graduation party. It has to be something more. Okay. That's why I'm here.

Crazy

In the middle of the school year. Looking at the gates of a boarding school. My mother hands me a letter. I'm supposed to give it to the headmaster later. By way of further explanation about me. I pick up a suitcase and wait for my father. He's still standing by the car, looking for something. I think I'm going to miss him. Sure we've fought a lot, but after a tough day at school he was always the first with a smile for me. We go up to the secretary's office. The boarding school looks even unfriendlier inside than out. Endless wood. Endless oldness. Endless rococo, or whatever—I'm as lousy in art history as I am in math. My parents like the building. They say the sound of our footsteps on the wooden floors is beautiful.

What do I know. There's a fat woman waiting for us in the secretary's office. She's called Angelica Lerch. She stands in front of me with her big fat cheeks and her big fat body. Makes me nervous. She gives me a couple of school stickers. Everything's covered with pictures of an eagle, grinning and clutching a schoolbag. Underneath is printed in cursive script: *Castle Neuseelen Boarding School—a new era in education.*

I'll give them to my parents; they can stick them up in the kitchen or God knows where. Angelica Lerch holds out her hand and welcomes me to the Castle. She herself has been here thirty years and has never had a single complaint. I decide not to comment. I sit down beside my parents on a copperish-colored settee and squash up closer to them than normal. I haven't done that for a long time. But it feels good; they're all warm, and it's like I'm protected. I take my mother's hand. Mrs. Lerch says the headmaster will be here in person in a minute to greet me. This said with a pinch of her nostrils. So. This is it—no way out. I'm sitting here and they'll come and get me soon. I feel shitty and stare at the floor. But I don't see the floor. I see . . . who cares what I see. I sit for maybe five minutes. Then the headmaster arrives. Jörg Richter is young, around thirty I guess, maybe a bit older. About six feet two inches. Black hair parted in the middle, friendly face. He comes in and drops into the next-best chair. Then, as if he'd forgotten, he jumps up again to greet us. His hand is damp. He asks us to come with him to his office. It's not far from the secretary's office. On the way I listen to the sound of the wooden floor. I don't think it's beautiful. So what?

The moment we reach his office, Mr. Richter gives me a couple of school stickers. They're more up-to-date than Mrs. Lerch's. The eagle is better designed and looks more three-dimensional. Even the schoolbag looks better.

All the same, I don't know what to do with them. I stick them in my mother's purse. Jörg Richter asks us to sit down. His office is big—bigger than the rooms I've seen so far. Bigger even than Mrs. Lerch's office. Expensive pictures on the walls. Fancy furniture. You could put up with things here. "So, Benjamin, looking forward to seeing your room?" asks Mr. Richter, raising his voice. I wonder how to answer this. For a long time I don't say a thing. Then I utter a dry "Yes." My mother nudges me. Oh, I forgot the letter. I pull it slowly out of my pocket.

"I've written you a short note," says my mother as she turns to the headmaster. "It's very important. Because my son hardly ever talks about things himself, I thought it would be best to write to you." The usual. Doesn't matter what school I go to; my mother thinks it's best to write a letter. As if you can sort out your problems that way. So okay. I dawdle over to the big desk in front of Mr. Richter. It's wood, like almost everything else here. Not to mention black as sin. Not much on it. A computer at one edge. The school logo, the eagle with the schoolbag, is carved into the surface. It's not easy to recognize, but I can make it out. I glance at the envelope.

Concerning my son, Benjamin Lebert's, partial paralysis, it says on it. How many times have I pushed this envelope into a teacher's hand? A dozen at least. Now I get to do it again. Jörg Richter reaches hastily for the envelope. His eyes glint with curiosity. He opens the letter. To my horror he reads it out loud. His voice is clear and full of understanding:

Dear Mr. Richter,
My son Benjamin has had a partial
paralysis of the left side of the body since
birth. This means that the functioning of the
left side of his body, particularly the arm and
the leg, is limited. In practical terms, this
means that he either cannot perform or has
difficulty performing such fine motor tasks as
tying his shoes, using a knife and fork,
drawing geometrical figures, using a pair
of scissors. In addition, he has problems
with sports, cannot ride a bicycle, and has
difficulty with any movement that involves a
sense of balance. I hope you will give him
your support by taking note of these things.
Many thanks. Warm regards,

Jutta Lebert

As the last word is read out, I shut my eyes. I want to be somewhere else, where explanations are superfluous. I slowly go back to my parents. They are standing by the wall, holding hands. You can see they're glad to have explained things. Jörg Richter looks up. He nods. "We will pay attention to Benjamin's handicap," he says. No questions.

We go up to my room. It's on the second floor, not far away. You go down a long wooden corridor that opens onto a long wooden staircase. The walls are snow white. We follow the headmaster upstairs. I hold my father's hand. Soon we reach another corridor.

"From now on you're at home here," says Jörg Richter. The walls are no longer white but yellow. It's meant to be an appealing yellow, but it misses. The floor is covered in gray linoleum. It doesn't go with the yellow walls. The corridor is empty. The other kids aren't back yet from winter vacation. Beside one of the windows is a plaque: THE TEACHER IN CHARGE OF THIS CORRIDOR IS LUKAS LANDORF, it says. ALL REQUESTS FOR MONEY FOR SHOPPING IN THE VILLAGE, ALL ISSUING OF POCKET MONEY, ALL REGULATION OF BEDTIMES AND AUTHORIZATIONS OF ANY KIND ARE HANDLED BY HIM. LUKAS LANDORF IS IN ROOM 219.

Mr. Richter points at the plaque. He twinkles. "Lukas Landorf will be your teacher, too. You'll like him. He's new here himself. Unfortunately, he won't be back from vacation for another couple of hours, but I know you'll have plenty of time to get to know him."

I look around for my father. He's standing behind me. He cuts a large figure. All strength. I don't want to see him go.

My mother is already inside. I follow her. It's a small room; it looked quite different in the brochure. The pale parquet floor is cracked and you can see holes in it. There's a bed squashed against each long wall. Both beds are old farmhouse style. In the middle there's a big flat desk with two chairs. One of them has a cushion with the eagle on it. Two cupboards for clothes against the wall. One of them's locked—the other must be for me. In addition, two nightstands and two storage cupboards, which seem to be meant to function as bookcases. Walls white. The only posters are above the bed on the left. Most of them fall into the category of sports or computer games. My roommate, who presumably put them up, isn't here yet. My father and Mr. Richter follow us into the room. Three suitcases and a bag are put down on the floor. I think about the secretary, Mrs. Lerch. Thirty years in this dump. Richter pulls open a drawer in the desk and fishes out a little plaque, four thumbtacks, and a hammer. He leaves the room and fixes the plaque to the door. Later I read: ROOM 211, JANOSCH ALEXANDER SCHWARZE (10TH GRADE) AND BENJAMIN LEBERT (9TH GRADE).

So now it's official. I'm stuck here. Possibly till I graduate. My parents are leaving. We say goodbye. I watch them go back down the corridor. Hear the doors creak. The footsteps on the wooden floors. The staircase. Mr. Richter goes with them. He has promised to be back soon. He has to talk over finances with my parents. Not my place. Hope I see them again soon. I take a bag and begin to unpack. Underwear, sweatshirts, sweaters, jeans. Where the hell is my checked shirt?

Janosch says the food is lousy. As in *lousy*.

As in seven days in the week. He's standing in the bathroom, washing his feet. I'm waiting. All the washbasins are in use. It's a big bathroom. Six washbasins, four showers. All tiled. All in use. Another five kids are waiting with me. The rest are asleep.

The floor is awash. No shower curtains. My feet are getting wet. With luck it'll be my turn soon. But things drag on. Janosch squeezes a pimple. Then washes his hands. When I get to the front of the line, I can't see a thing. The mirror's all fogged up—from the showers. Nice. Janosch waits for me. I decide I'd better be quick. I hastily brush my teeth and wash my face, then dry my hands. We leave the bathroom. It's only ten yards from our room. We go down the hall. Apparently it's known as Tarts' Alley, or Landorf Lane, after the teacher in charge. Sixteen kids live along here, all ages thirteen to nineteen. They're divided three to a room or two to a room, and there's one single room. This is for a particularly rough character called Troy—I can't remember his last name. Janosch talks about him a lot. Apparently he's weird, and he's been here a long time. A *long* time.

Our teacher in charge, Lukas Landorf, comes down Tarts' Alley. Not exactly a standout. A mop of black hair hanging down into his eyes. Old-fashioned glasses. He's a little taller than I am but not much. Janosch says Landorf never changes his green sweater. Apparently he's cheap—cheap as a Scot, according to Janosch—but otherwise a nice guy. Not too strict. Notices nothing. Even lets girls into the rooms. Human Valium. Some of the other teachers in charge are a lot more wide awake.

Lukas Landorf comes over to us. Smiles. He's got a young face. Can't be much more than thirty.

"So? Has Janosch shown you everything?"

"Yes," I say, "everything."

"Except the library," says Janosch. "We missed that. Can I show it to him now?"

"No you can't. Heavy day tomorrow. You guys have to get to bed." As he says that, he moves on. Looks a little wobbly on his feet. Must be missing his vacation already. Me too. Just a couple of days in South Tirol this time—that was it. Including a minor run-in with my older sister, Paula. But it was paradise, as I can see now.

We go into our room. Janosch wants to talk. It's this girl he's fallen in love with. Bonding seems to be a pretty quick process around this place. I've been here seven hours, and we're into girls already. Not my thing.

It's not just because I'm disabled. I've had about

as much luck with girls thus far as I've had in school, i.e., zip. The only thing I've been good at is eyeing them while the other guys nailed the ones I'd fallen for. I really had that down. Janosch talks and talks. I really feel sorry for the guy. He talks about flowers, blinding lights, and big tits. I can picture the whole thing and I'm with him all the way. A girl like that is something else. I sit down on the bed. My left leg aches, the way it does in the evening. It's been doing it for sixteen years. My bad leg. I can't count the times I've just wanted to amputate it and throw it away, along with my left arm. Why do I need either of them anyway? All they tell me is what I can't do — can't run, can't jump, can't be happy. But I've never actually done it—amputation, I mean. Maybe I need them to figure out math.

Or to fuck. If I want to fuck, I probably need my fucking left leg. Janosch by now is on to another subject—his childhood. He's saying that life used to be so great and it isn't anymore. And he says how cool it would be just to get out of this place and take off. Because it's about being free.

Janosch says the most important thing is being free. I know better than to say anything. First of all, I've only just got here. I'd like to take off too. No question—take off and run, and keep running. We smoke cigarettes. Against the rules, apparently, but so what.

Janosch lit mine with a match. I can't do it on my

own—takes two hands. If Lukas Landorf turns up, we'll throw them out the window. We're both sitting where we can do this. The window is wide open. Janosch looks at me. He's obviously tired. His eyes are deep blue and they look wet. The top of his bleach-blond head keeps nodding down toward the bedclothes. He gets up, stubs out the cigarette on the windowsill, and throws it out into the darkness of the parking lot. Just a few hours ago I was standing down there. Now I'm standing up above. In the center of things. Perhaps it's for the best. I throw my cigarette out too. Then we go to sleep. Or, rather, we try. Janosch talks about Malen, his girl. "She's unbelievably special." I'm impressed. Most kids I know say something else about their girls. Janosch just says she's special. That's it. It's great. I wish him luck with Malen. The night sky is clear and there's no moon. I sit at the window, the way I usually do.

I push myself up in bed, tired. It was an exhausting night. Not much sleep. A lot of sitting and waiting. Outside the sky is lightening. Maybe a sign. Then again, maybe not. Who knows.

The alarm clock goes off. A horrible noise that says *first day of school*. It also says *math*. It's also probably saying *you scored 6 again*. But I don't hear that yet. I turn it off. My black jeans and white PINK FLOYD—THE WALL T-shirt are ready. I put them on my side of the desk last night. My mother packed them both for me, right on top, next to my schoolbooks. What a surprise! I get dressed. I know where to go. Janosch showed me. He's still asleep. Maybe I should wake him. There are stiff punishments for sleeping in, apparently, but I know he knows this himself. I find a piece of paper in my pants pocket. I recognize my father's swooping handwriting:

Dear Benni,
I know this is a tough time for you. And I
also know that you'll have to rely on yourself
for lots of things. But please know that it's
all for the best, and be brave.

Papa

Be brave. It's all for the best. Nicely said. Really nice. Can't complain. I'll keep the note. Maybe show it to my children, so they can see what a big guy their father was, a really big guy. I stuff the piece of paper back in my pocket, then set off for breakfast. The dining hall is at the other end of the Castle. I head along Tarts' Alley, down the never-ending stairs to the main corridor, and eventually reach the headmaster's office. Then it's on through the official reception corridor, past Mrs. Lerch's room, down the stairs to the west wing, which lead directly to the dining hall. The west-wing stairs are old; with every step you take the wood groans and creaks as if it's begging for immediate relief. The dining hall is vast, with at least seventeen tables that seat a minimum of eight each. The walls have this beautiful paneling, and there are real paintings on them, showing wars, peace, love, and—no surprise here—eagles clutching schoolbags. I sit down at a table that's sort of squashed into a corner, and the only other kid sharing it with me is a sixth grader. The roll tastes dry. Every attempt to spread butter on it founders on my inability to hold it steady in my left hand. I keep trying but no luck. The roll shoots right across the table. A couple of girls sitting at a nearby table who've been following the action snigger. I'm ashamed. I retrieve the roll as quick as I can and ask the sixth grader to butter it for me. "So how old are you?" he asks. "Sixteen," I say. "By the time you're sixteen, you should have learned how to butter a roll," he says, and hands it back to me unbuttered. The girls snicker. I drink my tea.

"By the time you're sixteen, you should have learned to grasp a set square," asserts Rolf Falkenstein, the math teacher. He hands it back to me without having given me any help in drawing the proof of the theorem. Tough luck. So here I am on my first day of school. I shake my head. But everything started really well. The first classes, French and English, went fine, and I got through my famous fucking introductory aria. Usual thing. Come in and face the class, no idea where to stick your hands, and say:

Hi folks, my name is Benjamin Lebert, I'm sixteen, and I'm a cripple, just so you know. I thought it would interest you the way it does me.

Class 9B, which is the one I'm in, reacted the usual way: a couple of sideways glances, a little tittering, the first quick looks to size me up. For the boys I was now another of the nerds to be ignored, and for the girls I was just plain dead. Quite an achievement.

The French teacher, Heide Bachmann, says that here at Castle Neuseelen it doesn't matter whether anyone has a disability or not. What matters here at Neuseelen is loving, and hence binding values and social skills. Good to know. Class 9B isn't large: twelve kids, me included. Not like the state schools, where the minimum is around thirty-five. But they're not supposed to count. Here, we *count*. We count so much you can hear the place buckling under our psychic weight. We sit, like one big family, in a horseshoe facing the teacher. We love one another so much, we're practically holding hands. Boarding school as isolation chamber. One group, one circle of friends, one family. And Rolf Falkenstein, our math teacher, is our daddy. He's big. About six foot two. Pale face with prominent cheekbones. One of those guys who wear their age on their foreheads. Fifty—not six months' difference

one way or the other. Falkenstein's hair is greasy,
color nondescript, presumably gray, as far as I can
figure out. His fingernails are long and a mess. He
scares me a bit. He smacks his big set square against
the blackboard and draws a line, straight through a
geometrical structure. I think it's some sort of a base-
line. I try to copy it. Can't do it. The set square keeps
slipping off to the side. Finally I do it freehand. The
result is a sort of mathematical cartoon, more like a
kite than a straight line. After class Falkenstein calls
me aside. "You need some remedial coaching," he
says. "About an hour a day, I'd say." I can feel the joy.
"Okay. If that's what it takes." I leave.

Chapter 2

In the afternoon I go into the village with the other kids. It's not far. Homework today comes later. Even Troy comes with us. He plods along behind without saying a word. Now and again I turn around to him.

"Troy, what're you doing?"

"Nothing."

"You have to be doing *something*."

"No I don't."

I leave him in peace. His big bulky presence remains behind me. I see the black spikes of his hair out of the corner of my eye. We stop to have a smoke. *We* means everyone: Janosch, Fat Felix, Skinny Felix, Troy, and little Florian from eighth grade, a.k.a. Girl. "So, how was your first day?" he asks, drawing on his cigarette. His eyes water and he coughs.

"It went."

"*It went* means it was shitty?"

"*It went* means it was shitty."

"Same with me. The Reimanntal woman says I have to write out the house rules three times."

"You going to do it?"

"Do I look like I'm going to do it?"

No, he doesn't. His green eyes are ablaze, and he looks pissed off. His hair is a dark brown mop. He stares off into the distance and begins to frown.

I find myself thinking about home. The best place in Munich. A good hour's drive from here—not so far but out of reach all the same. Nothing special, really. A blue brick building on a little flat street, surrounded by two playing fields. But it's still the best place in Munich. What would I be doing now if I were there, not here? Reading, writing, napping. Maybe helping my mother with the dishes. Or maybe helping Paula, my sister, who's gay, with her newest conquest: Sylvia, the daughter of the folks next door. We would have to be careful, because it wouldn't be so smart if my parents found out. They're very sensitive about stuff like this. But I'm not there—I'm here, which is to say in boarding school, or rather sitting on some steps in a village.

I'm sitting talking to Florian a.k.a. Girl. He takes another drag on his cigarette and coughs. Louder this time. Janosch comes over.

"Girl can't hold her smoke, but it's no big deal. Not there yet, but tomorrow's another day." He laughs, then sits down next to me on the steps and pops a can of beer. We've put Troy on guard. He's standing up front by an elder bush. If a teacher or dorm supervisor shows up, he'll give the alarm. Otherwise the penalties are heavy—grounded for as much as a week and who knows what else. Smoking and drinking are punished the worst.

Janosch taps me on the shoulder. "What's up? Are you obsessing about this stupid disability thing? Chill out, we're all disabled. Look at Troy! Besides, you could have had it worse. Just because your left side's a mess is no reason to shit in your pants."

"I wasn't thinking about being disabled, I was thinking about being home. But thanks anyway."

"About being home? I can't help you there either. We all want to go home, but no luck. We're stuck here, like chunks of meat in a can of dog food. All swimming around in the same shit. And Fat Felix over there is the fattest chunk of all."

I get up slowly, and go over to Fat Felix. He's pissed off. "Forget it," I say, "he doesn't mean it."

"Of course he doesn't mean it, but he could still keep his mouth shut. It's not my fault I'm so fat, just like I'm sure it's not Troy's fault over there that he can't ever get a word out. That's us."

"True."

"Know what I think?" Skinny Felix interrupts.

"What?" asks Janosch.

"I think we're heroes."

"Heroes?" says Florian a.k.a. Girl. "Why heroes?"

"Because women can't leave us alone," says Felix. "Fat, crippled, silent, dumb. We're exactly the types women can't leave alone, you know?"

"Haven't noticed so far," says Fat Felix. "Women

hang around big blond guys who do stuff and could be in the movies. Like Mattis. Do you think women would hang around fat guys like me?"

"Mattis is a snake," growls Janosch. "They'd do better to hang around a fat guy like you. Or Benni. Look at Benni! Just the type women go for! Short brown hair, blue eyes, no fat on him. Born female idol!"

For a second I enjoy the general attention. "That's all you know," I say. I look down at myself. Still wearing my PINK FLOYD—THE WALL T-shirt and black jeans. Feet in Pumas with Velcro straps. They were white once; now they're somewhere between gray and black. They're the only shoes I can wear, because I can't tie shoelaces. Janosch says that's no reason to shit in my pants, but I still don't feel comfortable with the sneakers. Probably just have to get used to them. I take a slug of beer.

We head down to the village square. I'm sorry for them all in different ways, all five of them. Take Fat Felix. Only child of a brutal family, according to Janosch. Never had many friends. Just lots of candy. He's a slave to candy. Everyone calls him Glob or Obelix. He hates it but can't defend himself. The names have stuck to him since he started school and they'll still be sticking to him the day he manages to go home, having graduated. Which he will some-day. Fat Felix is good in school—3.7 grade average every year, no problem. He's even good at math, according to Janosch. But don't ask him to be your study partner after hours—supposedly he demands payment in candy. There's no actual proof, though. Aside from that, Felix is meant to be a good sport and a good friend. Hates wars, hates fights, probably not least because he always draws the short straw.

Next to Felix is baby Florian a.k.a. Girl. Per Janosch, he's frail and hypersensitive. Lost his parents in a car crash when he was six; since then he doesn't say much and usually only when you talk to him directly. He's been here since sixth grade and spends vacations in Hohenschäftlarn with his grandmother, who smothers him with affection till he almost can't take it anymore. He's one of the few kids here whose parents or relatives aren't rich. He's only in this school courtesy of the Department of Child Welfare, but he's still managed to settle in quite well.

About Skinny Felix there's not much to report. He's apparently as new here as I am. He came in three weeks ago; since then he's more or less inserted himself into the group, says Janosch. He's apparently a really nice guy and hasn't done anything to hurt anyone so far.

Troy's last, and Janosch calls him the rock that holds up Neuseelen. He's now in twelfth grade, having been here eight years. His life is one big silence. Nobody knows what goes on there. There's a rumor he has a dying brother. Nothing about the parents, nothing about the family.

Which leaves Janosch. My roommate. In the tenth grade, sense of humor. Always laughing and making noise. I haven't a clue about his family. Fat Felix says his father is some stock-market millionaire. But nobody knows for sure. Maybe I'll find out in due course.

We cross the market square. It's practically empty—very few of the stalls turn a profit these days. Florian buys himself a beer, keeping an eye out for any tutor who might be coming our way, and hastily sticks the can in a plastic bag, then comes running back to us. "I've heard a sex therapist is doing the rounds, and they say she's here now in Dr. Beerweiler's office. Apparently you can just walk in and talk to her. I bet my beer mug you don't dare to go in there right now, Janosch."

"Why would I bother? My sex life's been shit and still is shit. No therapy queen's going to fix that."

"You don't have to talk a lot," says Florian. "Just say you're gay and your tutor isn't exactly thrilled."

"Well, why would he be?" says Fat Felix.

"Besides," says Florian, "think of the prize. You always wanted a beer mug like that. Worth making yourself an idiot for, huh?"

"Girl, you're a jerk-off." Janosch is roaring with laughter.

Crazy

"I know," says Florian, "but at least I'm not a *gay* jerk-off."

So we all march off to the office of the local GP, Dr. Beerweiler. He's at the far end of the village and we have to cut through streets and alleys that are so narrow almost no cars can use them. There's practically zero traffic. The boys are excited, and they're all talking among themselves, throwing around suggestions and advice. Janosch stays cool. Draws on his cigarette. Seems nothing can unsettle him. We reach the house where the offices are. Ridiculous pile—art nouveau. The windows are filthy. It smells of doctors' offices before you even reach the front door. To the right is a brass plaque:

DR. JOSEF BEERWEILER, M.D.

CONSULTING HOURS—
MON–FRI 8 A.M.–2:30 P.M.

Under this is a flyer:

SEX ETC.
Advice for young people and adults who enjoy sex.
We are sharing Dr. Beerweiler's offices
from Jan 3–Jan 12.
Free consultations without previous appointment
eight hours daily.

Next to the text is a drawing of a boy holding his dick and laughing. In a balloon above his head it says

Homosexuals welcome here too.

Florian a.k.a. Girl points to the balloon—"You see, just right for Janosch"—and pushes him through the door. We follow them. The offices are on the first floor. No stairs to climb. That's a plus. Climbing stairs always hurts, and that's not on my wish list right now. Janosch rings the bell. There's a loud creaking noise and the door opens on its own. We go in. Plain smooth painted blue wooden floor, blinding white walls.

Reeks of doctors' offices. We have to go down a long corridor to get to the reception area. A young woman, blond, well-tended skin, silver glasses, is sitting at a desk.

"Can I help you?" Cold eyes. Looks stressed out. Janosch steps up.

"We're—I'm looking for the 'sex etc.' consulting room."

"Second on the left." As she says this, her voice rises.

She's sexy. I'm glad I met her, and decide to come back here on my own. Maybe a bit better dressed. Maybe bring a flower or something. Later. Not now. We reach a brown door that says SEX ETC. Fat Felix laughs and his ears turn red. Nervous.

"Anyone got anything to eat? Whatever. I could use something right now."

"Shut up, Glob," is the universal response. Janosch knocks. A refined voice answers, "Come in." The voice sounds to me to be around thirty-four. Maybe a little younger. We go into a small room. Everything's crammed together. Almost no room for us. Reddish-brown desk, nice shape, would fit right in my room at school, and behind it another blonde. A few wrinkles. She must really be thirty-four. Amazing green eyes, which you notice right away. Apart from that, pale. Three black leather chairs in front of her desk. Porno shots on the walls. Most of them missionary position or women giving blow jobs to big-muscled men. Skinny Felix and I are both interested. The blonde gets up.

"I'm Katherina Westphalia. We'll certainly get to know each other better. Are you from Castle Neuseelen?"

"Yes," says Fat Felix, mooning over a jar of Gummi Bears on the side table. "Do you think I could have one?" he asks politely.

"Of course," says Westphalia.

Janosch and I shake our heads.

"And what is your desire?" asks Westphalia.

Janosch turns to Florian.

"Mug's mine?" he whispers.

"Mug's yours," says Florian.

Janosch turns back to Westphalia and says, "I have only one desire." Now he's turning red too.

"What's your name?"

"Janosch."

"And what exactly is your desire?"

Fat Felix grins and stuffs a Gummi Bear into his face. The tension mounts. Everyone's staring at Janosch.

"Well," he says finally, and looks around. "I'm gay, and I'd like to have sex with Troy"—pointing at him. "But I'm afraid our tutor will catch us. How would he react? Or rather: How's a tutor supposed to react? Suspension? Three weeks waiting tables? Why the hell can't gays just be gay, huh, Troy?"

Janosch is in flying form, no shit. He's won the mug. He couldn't care less what Ms. Westphalia there thinks of him. Nor could he care less if she calls our tutor. He's the greatest, he's won a mug, and his friends will love him for life. Nothing bad can ever happen to him.

"How do you feel about that, Troy?" asks Westphalia.

Troy doesn't say a thing.

"Is he embarrassed?" she asks, turning to Janosch again.

"Of course he's embarrassed. I mean, just look at him. Who wouldn't be embarrassed?"

Crazy

Troy takes a step to the right. He's clearly absolutely furious. His eyes squeeze shut. You can feel he wants to scream; you can see it. But he can't do it. The scream tails off inside him. Fat Felix goes over to him.

"Pay no attention," he says. Exactly what I said to him myself just now. Maybe it'll help. Troy still doesn't say a word, but his face looks a little less black. It's a start. Janosch doesn't even notice. He's happily listening to Westphalia's advice and suggestions. He's grinning.

Half an hour later when it's over and we're standing in the market square again, Fat Felix opens his mouth.

"Can I ask something?"

"Ask," says Janosch.

"Why did we do that?"

"Because Janosch wanted my mug," says Florian. "You know that already."

"Your mug? That whole thing for your stupid mug? We could have just hung around and done nothing."

"Doing nothing would be boring," says Janosch. "Just think about it! Hanging around forever? I'd rather go and listen to Westphalia make suggestions. Even if the whole thing's for a stupid mug. I think that's what God intended."

"No, God didn't," says Fat Felix. "Do you really think God intended us to visit a sex therapist?"

"Of course he did. We're adolescents. And adolescents have to learn how to fuck."

"God doesn't have any extra time for fuckers," says Felix.

"But he does for jerk-offs?" the other Felix wants to know.

"If he doesn't, I've blown the whole thing." He starts to laugh. Everyone laughs. Even I laugh. But I don't think it's that funny. You can see Felix is serious.

"You don't really believe in the big bearded guy in the sky, do you?" asks Janosch.

"Yes," says Fat Felix. "I believe in him. And he's certainly a nicer guy than you are. He doesn't take the piss out of people. Everyone's equal to him. You take the piss out of everybody. Just look at Troy and me."

"I take the piss out of everybody," says Janosch. For the first time it gets to him. He sighs. "People never notice when I'm being serious and when I'm kidding around."

"I guess people should," says Felix, and pinches his nostrils. "Huh, Troy?"

I sit on the john and squeeze my eyes shut. I've got the runs. Maybe it's the food. But maybe it's the memory of an exhausting day. No idea. They keep yanking open the doors and throwing toilet paper at me.

"Piss-shit, piss-shit," comes the mocking call from out there. They're singing. Five minutes till study time. I'll never make it. So okay. I expect there'll be trouble. Nothing I can do about it.

I hate the toilet on Tarts' Alley, but it's the only one we've got. It's old and there are no locks. Almost all the tiles have already been broken out. There are puddles of urine on the floor. The Landorf guys don't care where they piss. When they have time, they also piss at the ceiling. Fun.

Heide Bachmann the French teacher is in charge today. She glances up as I come in. She's been buried in a book.

"It's not such a good idea to arrive late for study hall on your first day at school," she says. Her voice is husky. Her brown hair wobbles and her eyes are angry.

"I know. I'm sorry, but . . ."

"Sit down!" she says and makes a note in the class book. "No, not there! Next to Malen, please."

I do as ordered and go to Malen. Janosch's dream girl. She's sitting over to one side of the classroom, squashed between two single desks. One of them is occupied by Malen's friend Anna. Her long blond hair is pinned up. Pale face, but a friendly one. She glances up at me and smiles. I smile back. The second desk is free. I sit down. There's a screeching noise as I push the chair back. Everyone looks. Malen too. She laughs. She's incredibly beautiful. I understand Janosch. Her skin is bright and soft. Gentle eyes. A smile to die for.

"Can you help me with math?" she asks, crossing one leg over the other. I swallow. "No, unfortunately, I can't. I wish I could understand it myself." She nods and turns away. I look at her tits. Well, that was my big chance. Here one minute, gone the next. The usual. I look at my exercise book. Even more joys in store:

Math
Physics
English
French

Everything's due tomorrow. Not to mention a music report and a discussion on youth and alcohol. As if there weren't enough to do. I get to work.

Bachmann is on patrol. She looks pissed off. She comes and props herself on my desk. Without meaning to, I think of my last school: 3 Borscht-allee, Luitpold Park, Munich. Himmelstoss High School. I was there for three years. Stressful. Didn't make it in school or at other things. Three or four good essays, that's about it. It was everyone for himself. But then, after all the shit that washed over you in the morning, you got to go home. No monitored study hall, no Bachmann; one o'clock and you were out of there. See your mother. Cry. Laugh. Hope. Can't do that here. Here you have to stay till you're black in the face. It goes on and on. Malen stands up. She wants to copy down one of Ms. Bachmann's notes. She comes over to my desk with her math book open. Her shoulder-length blond hair is pulled back and her red blouse lets you see a lot. So does her short skirt. She bends over my shoulder. I feel fantastic. If I were a man, it might take a bit more to impress me, but I'm a kid, and when you're a kid, someone bending over you is enough. Bachmann signs off on the math exercise. I wish I were that far along. But I have a whole theorem still to do.

"You seem to have settled in," says Bachmann, chewing a fingernail.

"Yes I have. Quite well so far." I think of my parents. And Janosch.

"Good," she says. "It would still be better to be on time next time. Things like that can get unpleasant after a while."

I'll bet.

Her backside wobbles back to the big desk up front. I watch her go. Then I concentrate on the theorem.

Chapter 3

At supper there are vanilla croissants. Nice. A lot of kids from tenth, eleventh, and twelfth grade went off on a trip to some art exhibition, so there's more for us. Fat Felix brought spare bags with him—he wants to grab a couple of croissants and take them upstairs. We hide the bags under the table, and at regular intervals we go for second helpings. Nobody notices. Florian has even hunted up some cocoa from somewhere. Rare event, says Janosch. And to round things off, there's fruit. We're in bliss. Even Troy laughs. He takes another croissant. Outside it's snowing, and hailstones fling themselves noisily against the big window.

"So, guys," says Janosch. "How about we go visit the girls tonight?" As he says this, he turns toward our tutor, Lukas Landorf, who's sitting at the table opposite, and grins.

"I'm not going anywhere with you again," says Fat Felix, biting into his apple.

"Don't be so thin skinned," says Janosch. "I didn't mean it."

Crazy

"That's what Benni said to me too, but it doesn't help."

"What d'you mean, Benni said it to you already?" asks Janosch.

"Because Benni's cool," says Florian a.k.a. Girl.

"He's right," says Janosch. "Benni's really cool. Huh, guys—is Benni cool or what?"

"Benni's cool," they say, and punch my shoulder.

I think about my sister. I miss her. What's she doing right now? Probably hanging around some lesbian event in the old town. I know these. She's taken me to a couple of them herself, secretly of course. We climbed out the window and my parents never knew a thing. Just as well, they wouldn't have understood. So it was us two, and I had such a great time. Usually I was the only guy. And unlike other guys, I got on with the girls. I didn't stink, didn't booze, didn't belch, and I didn't indulge in "rituals of humiliation designed to degrade women." I could stay. Sometimes the whole night. Then my sister would bring me home. She was the heroine of the evening. Everyone liked her. Everyone thought she was beautiful. But she's really small, maybe five feet two inches. She always wears her brown shoulder-length hair in a ponytail. She has an open, unlined face. Expressionless. Almost never cries. Or laughs. Always a blank. Shit, I love her.

"So what about the women?" says Janosch.

"So what about them?" says Florian.

"Well, are we going to go visit or not?" Janosch sounds pissed off.

"So what are we gonna do when we get there?" asks skinny Felix. "I bet it's gonna be a replay of the mug thing—"

"The mug thing was *crazy*," Janosch interrupts.

He's always saying *crazy*. Anything excites him, he says *crazy*. He loves the word. "That thing was crazy?" says Fat Felix in amazement. "So was it crazy to call me a big fat chunk of dog food?"

"No. That wasn't crazy, that was an accident." Janosch laughs.

"I'll land a couple right on your nose, then we'll talk about a real accident," says Felix.

"Does that mean you're not coming with us?"

Glob throws a croissant at him.

Janosch turns around, still laughing. "So what about you guys? Glob's in."

There's a general mumble of *We're in*. I mumble along with them. That's what you're supposed to do.

"Good," says Janosch. "I'll take care of the girls— you take care of the beer. Meet Lebert and me in our room at twelve-fifty a.m."

It must be around ten o'clock. I don't know exactly. It's pitch black outside. I sit on the windowsill and look out.

Janosch sits next to me and smokes.

Crazy

"Can you tell me something, Janosch?" I ask.

"I can tell you lots of things."

"I'm not interested in lots of things. Just one thing—what's it like not to be disabled? Not weak? Not empty? What's it feel like to run your left hand across a table? Does it feel alive?"

Janosch thinks. He runs his left hand across the windowsill.

"Yes, it feels alive." He swallows and pulls on his cigarette. A red dot glows in the middle of his face.

"And how does that feel?"

"It feels like life," he says. "No different really from when you run your right hand across it."

"But it feels great, doesn't it?"

"Never thought about it. But that's the thing: life's something like *never having to think about it.*"

"Never having to think about it?" I'm furious. "Do you really believe nobody ever thinks about what we're doing?"

"Not down here, for sure," says Janosch. "If anywhere, up there. And who knows, maybe our good friend Glob's right about his big bearded guy in the sky."

"Would you repeat that to him later?"

"Of course not," says Janosch. We don't say any more. Outside it starts to snow again.

"I don't want to be disabled," I whisper. "Not like this."

"So how?" Janosch looks over at me questioningly.

"I want to know who I am. Everyone knows that much: a blind man can say he's blind, a deaf man can say he's deaf, and a cripple can damn well say he's a cripple. I can't. All I can say is I'm partially disabled or partially spastic. What does that sound like? Most people just think I'm a cripple. But the few left over think I'm perfectly normal. And I can tell you that somehow causes even more problems."

"Don't shit in your pants," says Janosch. "As far as I can see you're not disabled and you're not normal. Far as I can see, you're crazy." He laughs. "Uh-huh—you're not disabled, you're crazy."

"Crazy?"

"Crazy!"

Now we're both laughing. It feels good, and we can't stop.

"So which girl do you want to visit?" I ask when we've finally calmed down. "Malen, I guess?"

"Of course it's Malen. You didn't think I meant Florian? Right. Malen is in a triple room. The rest of you can have the other two."

Janosch's eyes cloud over. I can see the love in them. I have to tell him. Now. It's time. Let's hope he takes it well. I open my mouth and raise my voice. "I'm afraid I have something to tell you."

"What?"

"I think I've got a thing for Malen." Suddenly, spontaneously, I start to laugh again. "Are you going to kill me?"

That sets Janosch off again, almost louder than before.

"Crap."

"Crap?" I say happily. "You mean you don't mind?"

"No. Of course I mind. But you should know that at least a hundred fifty guys in this Castle have got a thing about Malen, so one more or less doesn't matter much. Besides, you're only half grown. Crazy but half grown." He's in hysterics now, clutching his stomach and sobbing with laughter, while I'm imitating the whole thing. His eyes start to roll. Finally when he gets over to the windowsill he starts to calm down and then goes to get a couple of cans of beer out of his chest. He drinks one at a single gulp and gives me the other.

"How do I look?" he asks.

"Good."

He stands there in front of me, my roommate Janosch Schwarze. Sixteen years old. Tenth grade, high school. Supposed to be good at math. Maybe I should get him to coach me. But that's not what it's about right now. Besides, we're not a good match according to Mr. Landorf. Maybe we'll try it anyway. I think we get on.

What was it Janosch said just now? Got it—life is *never having to think about it.* So we won't.

Chapter 4

"Say something!"

"What?"

"Anything!"

Janosch is in bed with the cover pulled over his head, but his blue eyes are still visible in there. I'm sitting on the edge of the bed so that he can stick his feet out the way he likes. There's still time to wait, maybe another twenty minutes. Then they'll be here. I'm a little wound up. I'm worried about the dark corridors and our footsteps on the wooden floor. We've got a long way to go. If Janosch wasn't kidding, we also have to use the fire escape to get to the girls' corridor, which is one floor higher. All the doors are locked at this hour. Which means we have to use the window. Everyday exercise for a cripple. Janosch opened the window a bit wider this evening. I wish one of the tutors had shut it. But I bet they haven't. Janosch is sure about this. He's almost asleep. I'm supposed to wake him. He said so himself. Twenty minutes before zero hour is when the urge to sleep is strongest. As a man, you have to be able to conquer it, he says, particularly when you're meeting girls. I can hardly keep my eyes open either. I try to light two cigarettes. Sometimes I can manage it. Janosch sits up. There's a *Playboy* on his bed. A couple of babes from the pop group Mr. President have stripped off. Not bad. We take a good look.

"D'you want to have children?" I ask Janosch as I size up Danii's and T's tits.

"I certainly want to have sex," says Janosch, "and if I have a child, then it can have sex too. I want to have sex and my child can have sex." He laughs.

"Janosch, I'm serious."

"Of course I want a child. Maybe even two." He draws on his cigarette. "I like children. I want to know what it's like when your son comes lurching over to you and mumbles, *Pa—I'm not drunk, you can trust me one hundred percent.*"

"That happen to you?"

"Of course it happened to me. That kind of thing is always happening to me. Maybe that's why I have such good relations with my parents?" Janosch is laughing all over again. Typical Janosch laugh—an upsurge, a cough, a flicker of the eyelids, a grunt. Except this time it seems a little tired. We bury ourselves in *Playboy*. It used to be we pinned up pictures of superheroes in our rooms. Now what we pin up is super tits. Really we're still small boys.

I think about my father. A nice guy. He's already

been my father for sixteen years. And I still don't understand him. He's some kind of amateur astronomer, at least that's what he says. He built himself an observatory at his mother's place out in the country. It's not large—a little black wooden hut on top of my grandmother's garage. But it's comfortable. Some nights when he goes out there he takes me with him. Usually weekends and holidays. That's when we talk about life. I don't understand a lot of what he says; he uses big words and technical terms.

But now and again I can see what he's getting at—for example, when he talks about *his* father. That he's in a lot of pain sometimes. That he smokes a lot. That the cancer is eating his lung away. And sometimes my father's just fighting with my mother. I can see what he's getting at there too, and I understand him. My father is well intentioned toward me, I know, which is reason enough for me to be well intentioned toward him. He likes the Rolling Stones—they're a rock group from way back. Every time they're on tour, he takes me. He hopes I'll like the music. I don't, but I still have a terrific time. I'm happy for my father, because he's happy, and I'm happy that we're being happy together. It's nice. I think the sky's meant to clear tonight.

"I wish I was with Victoria from the Spice Girls and we were fucking," says Janosch, pointing to a photo in *Playboy*. "She has such terrific tits."

"I'm not familiar with them."

"Neither's Fat Felix," says Janosch, "but that doesn't stop him from talking about them all the time. So don't worry about it."

Just at that moment, the door opens, and a big face peers in. It's undoubtedly attached to Fat Felix—the blond mop on top is unmistakable. As are the round cheeks. His ample body is stuffed into a pair of too-tight blue Tony the Tiger pajamas, which are trying but failing to contain his beer belly.

"So, you bums, did I miss something?"

"Just Victoria from the Spice Girls," says Janosch.

"Victoria from the Spice Girls?" Fat Felix is practically panting. "Where?"

"Here!" Janosch picks up *Playboy*. Felix speed-wobbles over, and behind him the room fills up with Florian, Troy, and Skinny Felix. They're all on tiptoe to avoid anyone hearing them. Nocturnal activities land you in deep shit around here.

"Look at those tits!" Glob is ecstatic and lifts the magazine to catch the light from the lamp on the night table.

"How would you know?" says Janosch. "And besides, she's out of your league. True, guys? Isn't she out of his league?"

"True—she's right out of his league."

Janosch laughs. "Usually there are two reasons

kids hate themselves. Either they're too fat or they've never had sex. Believe me, Felix, I share your pain."

Glob's had enough. He takes a running jump onto Janosch's bed. There's a scream. Covers and pillows start flying around and it turns into a fight.

Fat Felix doesn't have a chance. Janosch wipes up the floor with him, but he won't give up. He uses his legs to try and pin Janosch against the wall, which involves lifting them way up over his chest. It looks hopeless. He kicks out. His face is hidden but his big fat backside isn't. It's in full sight, and the pajama pants are in danger of splitting. Doesn't take long— two more minutes fighting and the elastic waistband gives way. His pants slide down and we're looking at his naked ass. We all start to laugh. The fighting cocks disengage.

"You could make it as a sumo wrestler," says Janosch, gathering up his scattered bedding.

"I know, but only when you get a job as a restroom attendant." He grins. He's holding his pajama pants against his hip with the second and third fingers of his right hand. "Can any one of you idiots tell me how I'm going to climb the fire escape with these?" His left hand points to the pajama bottoms.

"You're a grown-up," says Janosch loftily. "You can do it. A sumo wrestler could do it twice. Come on, Glob, make an effort!"

"Nobody asked me if I want to grow up. It's a lot easier not to, huh, guys?"

"Bag it," says Janosch. "We're not doing therapy here, we're talking beer and sex. It's not about our inner child."

"I'm tired," says Florian a.k.a. Girl.

"Who asked you?" says Janosch. "You said you're in, and you're in. Did you get the beer?"

"Troy has it," says Skinny Felix. "He has the biggest pockets. And he doesn't sing."

"He doesn't even talk, so why should he sing?"

"Search me," says Florian. "Anyhow, he's got the beer."

Janosch sighs. "Then we're all set. You okay, Benni?"

"All set."

So things start to roll. Another pointless event.

The same six of us. Janosch says these pointless events will single us out. As I look around, I see he's right. Here we all are—the pointless eventers. Florian a.k.a. Girl, in a rust-colored pajama top and white undershorts. His bare feet patter on the linoleum floor. He's often made night trips with Janosch to the girls' corridor. They really like him up there. He's made some kind of a move on Anna, Malen's friend. He's always making moves on people, according to Felix, sometimes three a week. Never has any luck. He's always the loyal sidekick, never the real lover. He'd be in a total panic if he were. But that doesn't stop his trying, as per Janosch's code of pointlessness.

Next to him is Fat Felix. Apparently he doesn't often go along on trips to the girls' corridor. Doesn't find it easy to talk to girls, according to Janosch. His eyes tear up and he talks complete crap—like soccer, for example. Janosch is sure soccer turns girls off. A bit like talking about pesticides. Which is why the others always make sure Felix has a lot to drink. That way, he falls asleep pretty quick, and when he's asleep, he can't talk garbage. At least that's Janosch's view. Felix has brought along a clothespin to deal with the fire escape. He clamps it onto the front of his pajama pants. As he moves, it moves in rhythm with him. Looks weird. As if he had a mouse in there.

Behind him are Skinny Felix and Troy. The two big question marks. Nobody knows much about them. Supposedly Troy hasn't even fallen in love with anyone yet. All he wants is quiet. His black spikes of hair are standing up every which way; otherwise he looks like he always does. Long clean-shaven face. No pimples, just a couple on his neck. Pale skin—looks as if it's never seen the sun. Apparently couldn't give a shit about nocturnal adventures: it's just he can't sleep. So he often goes along but spends most of the time sitting in a corner. Never says a word, and no one's ever shown a flicker of interest in him. He's just there. Like the moon or the stars. This is also Skinny Felix's first time, just like me. And he's all wound up, just like me. You can see it. His bare legs are trembling. He's wearing nothing but a pair of patterned undershorts. Nothing on his top half either. Felix is all muscle. His stomach's a washboard. Must be a come-on for Malen, I think. He's got a lot more to offer than I do.

Which brings us to the second last in our gang, namely Janosch. He's left his pajama top behind in the room too. After all, he has to keep up with the others. He's got nothing on but his wine-red pajama pants. They're scrunched up a bit. You can see his powerful calf muscles. He's borrowed a pair of glasses from Charlie, another one of Landorf's pupils. He wants to look more intelligent. I can't tell if he's succeeding. The glasses are narrow, with rectangular lenses. Black frames. Florian thinks that if it was up to Janosch, we'd be on the girls' corridor every night. Because he loves having fun. Gets a kick out of it. Besides which he hopes one of these times he'll finally get to see Malen's tits. Supposedly she promised him, one night, when he went up there on his own. Fat Felix says it's all bullshit— nobody promised him that. He can't see reality anymore because he's got tits on the brain. You have to work for tits, says Felix, they don't just fall into your hands. Certainly not when you're a small boy with bleached hair, a moon face, and jowly cheeks.

Impossible. Nonetheless, Janosch is the ringleader. And a big one. He'll keep the pack together. Kick everyone in the ass if necessary, says Felix. He's really good at that; he can do it. Beside him, crowded to one side, comes the last person in the group: me. I carefully keep putting one foot in front of the other. I scratch a fingernail along the wall. It's quite dark. I'm a little afraid. I've never done anything like this before — nocturnal activities and stuff like that aren't my thing. I'd rather be asleep. Janosch says I'm a lard ass. I can sleep all I want when I'm dead. Besides, I'll see Malen. And if I see Malen, I'll forget about sleep. He's probably right. I can visualize her friendly smile. Her hair. Her eyes. Will she be pleased I'm coming? Quite possibly she just wants to sleep. I wouldn't blame her. I find myself thinking about my own bed. And my parents. Asleep right now. My mother's bound to be dreaming about me — I'm sure of that. She always does when I'm away. She's probably wondering if I'm freezing or something. And she's certainly asking herself if I packed the bedspread, the brown one with white stripes. Probably also if I've shut the window, because if not I could catch cold. That's how my mother is. Always worrying about me. Probably why I'm such a wimp. With a normal kid it would be okay — he could balance things out. With friends. With books. With fooling around. But when you're disabled, it's hard. You tend to hide under your mother's skirts. Just resting. Breathing. Sleeping.

Yes, I'd say I'm a real mama's boy. Helpless. All I've got is my sister, who periodically drags me out into the night. And I've got Janosch, who says I shouldn't shit in my pants. I need them both if I'm going to stand on my own two feet. My mother too. Whom I love. Sounds dumb. But that's what they call growing up. So they say, anyway.

I keep putting one foot in front of the other. The other five are faster than me, quick and supple. I can't keep up. I go slowly, dragging along behind. My left foot is good at dragging. I can't lift it properly. Not strong enough. I'm barefoot, but the dragging still makes a racket. It echoes right along Tarts' Alley. Janosch turns around, mad. He frowns, then recognizes the problem, and comes back to me.

"I'll carry you on my back," he says apologetically. "Too much noise."

"Too much noise?"

"Yes, Landorf'll hear us. I'll carry you. You're slower than us anyway."

Everyone agrees, even Fat Felix.

"Will you carry me, too?" He turns to Janosch.

"You mean, to try out a new form of torture?"

"No. To carry me," says Felix.

"First thing you need to check is whether you're still carrying your pants properly," whispers Janosch.

He points at the clothespin on Felix's pajama bottoms, then he turns around and gets down on his knees. I'm standing behind him now. I look down at myself and grin. I'm wearing my father's pitch-black pajamas, which must be at least twenty years old. What it says on them is WHEN THE GOING GETS TOUGH, THE TOUGH GET GOING—an ancient piece of wisdom from rock 'n' roll. My father loves it, has for centuries. Probably no accident. My skin's a little damp, I'm shaking, and there's a foul taste in my mouth. There was lentil stew for lunch. Or maybe it's this evening's vanilla croissants. I must have eaten too many.

I squeeze my legs around Janosch's hips. Right leg no problem. Left leg big problem. Takes time. Felix and the others give me a hand. Janosch has to keep crouching for a bit. Then he stands up with a bit of a jerk that throws me into the air. I almost fall off, and quickly get my right arm around his neck. We march on. So here we go, the six of us. Night. Tarts' Alley. A moon. It's okay on Janosch's back. Better than having to walk. Things go very quickly, just a bit bumpily. I have to watch out for my head. The ceilings on Landorf's corridor are very low—take a jump off the floor and you can touch them. Janosch keeps himself bent way over. He's sweating a bit. But he's managing, all things considered. A man has to be able to take it, he says. The two Felixes wink at each other and grin. Florian is next to them, looking as if he could fall asleep along the way. Troy brings up the rear. His face is expressionless. He's stuffed the cans of beer under his pajama top. Even in this light you can see them quite clearly. They give him fabulous curves, but he seems not to care. I'm tired. My eyeballs keep drooping farther and farther. I'm thinking about bed. And Malen. And my parents. Asleep.

Chapter 5

"Does everyone do shit like this when they're young?" asks Fat Felix as we get to the end of Landorf's corridor.

We were extra quiet all the way along it. Janosch says the tutor sometimes is still up playing with his computer around this time of night. He's supposed to be nuts about poker. But it's only a rumor.

"What sort of shit?" asks Janosch.

"Going to visit the girls at night," says Felix. "Up the fire escape! Don't you know the penalty for unnecessary use of the fire escape?"

"Haven't a clue. And we've done it a thousand times before—why're you getting so excited? We're heroes, or did you forget? Your namesake said so."

"My namesake's a jerk-off," says Felix. "What does he know?"

"Exactly," says Florian a.k.a. Girl. "What do *any* of us know? That's what makes us heroes. Heroes never know anything, and as heroes we can do anything we like. A fire escape isn't going to get in our way."

"Is that the logic of youth?" asks Glob.

Crazy

"No, it's the logic of jerk-offs," says Skinny Felix.

"The logic of jerk-offs and heroes," adds Janosch. Faint sniggering echoes along the connecting corridor, maybe even reaches down Tarts' Alley to the tutor's door. But nobody's paying attention. We carry on. I'm beginning to feel like an idiot on Janosch's back. As if I can't manage for myself or walk on my own. But I can. Or at least I always could. But I don't say anything to him; he'd only tell me again not to shit in my pants. And I'm not up to making trouble right now. Through the window I look at the sky. A great black expanse, with a scattered cargo of bright stars. Looks nice. Hard to believe some of them don't even exist anymore, since they've been dead for aeons; it's just we don't see them because the light takes too long to get here. On the horizon you can see the Alps, just dark shapes, darker than the sky. Hannibal crossed them, as our history teacher was always telling us. I have to admit I kept dozing off and dreaming. That was around the time I got a crush on this girl in my class. Isabel. She was incredibly pretty, with dark hair. Always wore a tight T-shirt that was glued to her skin everywhere except where it dipped in front, so anyone could cop a look down there. It was great. She said she didn't feel a thing for me. I was too weird. Besides, she was hooked on Marco, who was a good friend of mine. The two of them became a couple. They once got it on in the girls' lavatory during the summer party. I had to stand outside and keep guard.

It was a thrill. Your youth is the happiest time of your life, I think. Not just school but all the other stuff. Unbeatable experiences. The old guys are right. I can't remember a time when I didn't have a crush on somebody. I thought girls were great even way back in kindergarten. But I also can't remember a time when I went out with anyone. I'm too weird, as Isabel would put it. So what the hell is *weird*, anyhow? Is it weird to set off on your friend's back on a night pilgrimage to the girls? Not to mention up the fire escape. Not to mention with Troy. And Florian a.k.a. Girl. Is it weird for Fat Felix to be wearing a clothespin so his pajama pants don't fall down? Is Janosch just weird, or is he some kind of weird hero? I wish I didn't give a shit, and then I could go back to thinking about superheroes again. They're simpler. It's hard to figure out girls. *They're* the weird ones.

The other five guys come to a halt at the end of the corridor. There's a big window in front of them. Skinny Felix opens it. "We're here."

"The fire escape?" I ask.

"Fire escape," says Janosch.

He bends over to let me down and wobbles a little. Seems about to lose his balance. But he makes it. I can dismount. I have a funny feeling in my legs.

Crazy

As if I hadn't walked in ages. My back is cold. My pants are sticking to my rear end. I go over to the window and take a look. Janosch, Florian, and the two Felixes join me. They stare out and smoke. Points of red light glow in the darkness. Troy's behind them. You can hardly see him. His face is in deep shadow. I turn my attention back to the window. It's more of a glass door. At least one man can get through there. Which is what's supposed to be the case, since it's an emergency exit. The casement window moves in the wind. Seems to be blowing like crazy out there. Skinny Felix shouldn't have opened it yet. The others are still smoking. It's cold. I'm not smoking; I can do that upstairs. Besides which I have to take care that I don't start overdoing it. I smoke quite a lot for a sixteen-year-old. Marlboros, of course. Only idiots smoke Camels, says Janosch. And we're not idiots. My parents always maintain I don't smoke. They'd keel over if they knew, my mother in particular. She's in alternative medicine. She says even one cigarette can cause terrifying damage. And she smokes herself. I don't get it. But that's how it is with my parents. They keep forbidding me things they either do themselves or used to. Maybe that's why they fight so often. It's been getting really bad recently. As the son, you just feel helpless. Empty. It hurts. I often wish they'd separate, then I wouldn't have to deal with all the shit. But I'm also glad I've got them both as support. And as friends. As family, in fact. It's all so much crap, but it gets to me; I can't shake it. Doesn't matter where I am. I love my parents. As a couple, not apart. Holidays together. Good times. Christmas. And fights. More and more fights. Sometimes it's about my upbringing. Sometimes it's about their own upbringing. And sometimes it's just about who should take the goddamn empties back to the supermarket. According to my sister that's the only reason I got sent off to boarding school: to spare me the fights. Now she's the one who has to put up with them. All on her own.

I haven't called home so far. Probably because I'm afraid of my weeping mother. My sister's at her wits' end. My worried father. When I was still at home, I always tried to look on the bright side. Nice weather. Good TV program. Being together. I often just swallowed the fights. I still catch myself tuning them out.

Perhaps that's a good thing. But it gets harder and harder. The whole thing's for shit. And now I've got to climb a fire escape. When I stick my head out the window, the wind blasts into my face and whips my short hair around. The inner courtyard is lit by a small lamp. It's always on at night, according to Florian. To help the tutors when they're out *checking*. *Checking*, in Neuseelen language, means being caught while up to something illegal. Janosch says *getting checked* is uncrazy. He laughs. The fire escape is a little to one side of the window. Just where you can reach it with a jump to the right. Bottom line is that means I can't get there. I don't jump. Let alone a big jump. Not even when there's a fire. And I'd rather burn up than jump.

Janosch, Felix, and the others flick their cigarette butts down into the inner courtyard. They take a step forward. Janosch sets his right foot on the windowsill and climbs up, the open cigarette pack held between his thumb and forefinger. He lets it drop into his pajama pants, where it makes a rectangular shape against his right side. Sits well. Doesn't even move when he moves. Janosch is all prepared for the jump.

"Crazy, huh?" he asks triumphantly.

"Not crazy, dumb." Fat Felix is pissed off. It's the old song. The two of them collide. As always.

"Crazy and dumb are essentially the same thing anyway," Janosch whispers, and laughs.

"Essentially—no. In reality—yes," is Glob's retort. "And in reality I'm not going up that fire escape again."

"Me neither." I add my whisper to the conversation.

"But essentially you're going to do it, yes?" is what Janosch wants to know. He's won—it's over. Further arguments don't count. Our leader has kicked us in the ass. Fat Felix still tries to disobey orders, but he's cracking up.

"What if my pants fall down?" he asks despairingly.

"Then this dump of a courtyard will finally have something to look at. It would be great. When the headmaster drags the new kids in here every day to show them around, he tells them they've really got something to see. So show it to them!"

Everyone laughs, even Troy, who's come out of his corner.

The beer is still hidden under his pajama top. It must be warm by now. Janosch waves me over to him on the windowsill. He thinks we should jump one after the other. Like two real heroes. When he gets onto a rung of the ladder, he can pull me over to him without any problem. I don't have to take a real jump. All the same, I'm afraid. I can't explain it. Sweat breaks out on my forehead. My knees are trembling. The drop is more than thirty feet. Janosch jumps. In a fraction of a second he's hanging on the ladder. His feet grope for the lowest rung. It takes more than half a minute for him to secure his footing. He waves.

"I'm afraid of heights. What if I fall?"

"You won't fall. And if you do, I'll catch you. I'm here. And if Fat Felix can get his ass in gear, so can you."

Crazy

Glob sticks his head out the window. He's blushing. "I'll get more than that in gear, but not till I'm upstairs."

"Sweetheart, I know that," says Janosch. "So—Benni, you can get going."

Okay. It can't be that hard. I jump. There's a short period when I'm hanging in the air. Then I seize Janosch's hand. He guides me safely to a rung of the ladder. We climb a little higher. Florian jumps. He needs space. My left side has problems in store. I should add that I never climb anything. I only have to see a ladder and I panic. My left foot keeps getting caught in the rungs of the ladder. My left hand keeps losing its grip. The higher I go, the worse it is. I'm very high now. Barefoot, of course. The ladder's made of steel. Each step on the round rungs hurts. With luck I'll be at the top soon. All this just for the girls, I think. Some people would say I'll never need a girl. And on my second night, here I am hanging desperately off a castle wall, trying to get to them. That's the way it is, according to Janosch. It's right. We need girls, that's all. Like light or oxygen. All of us. Even Glob. Why, God knows. Now Glob jumps. One hand is clutching his pants, the other a rung of the ladder. He gives a sigh of relief. Does Troy need girls too? It's his turn to jump. It doesn't seem to be much of a problem for him. We're all here. Janosch thinks Troy will get interested in the girls. He has to. After all, he thinks Uma Thurman is sensational.

Although in Florian's opinion she's lacking in the chest department. The only time she looked really good was in that skintight costume in *Batman*. Next to the fire escape there's a plaque. I climb past it. It's set into the stone with four silver nails. The plaque itself is bronze.

THIS IS A FIRE ESCAPE

MISUSE OF ANY KIND IS PUNISHABLE BY LAW

I swallow.

Okay. I'll soon be at the top. I see the window in the girls' corridor. Janosch has almost reached it. It's open. The casement is moving in the wind. Janosch grabs for the windowsill.

"I've got a question," says Skinny Felix as we pull him into the girls' corridor. He's shivering a bit, twitching here and there. Maybe he should have been wearing more.

"So ask," says Janosch encouragingly, shoving his glasses back up on his nose. They'd fallen down his face during the climb.

"Do you think anyone's been tracking all this? And if they have, will they praise us later for being so brave?"

He means it. He sounds preoccupied. Maybe also

a touch of skepticism in his voice but fundamentally genuine. Skinny Felix is smart. I don't often hear him kidding around. Glob says he's our philosopher. I think he's right, there.

"Who do you mean in particular?" asks Florian a.k.a. Girl.

"God, maybe. Do you think anyone up there watches us?"

"Nobody watches us," says Florian.

"So why are we doing all this shit then?" is what Felix wants to know.

"Maybe just because nobody's watching," says Girl.

"But shouldn't that make us all shit-scared of life?" is Felix's next question.

"Well, we are," says Janosch. "Every step is a struggle."

"You looked pretty casual hanging off that ladder," says Glob.

"I won't achieve everything I want, but I'm going to try everything I can," is Janosch's retort.

"What's that got to do with fear of life?" says Glob.

"A great deal. Don't ask me why. Maybe the constant feeling of wanting to achieve something."

"Have you achieved anything yet?" I ask.

"Come on! I just climbed the ladder with you and Glob! You think that's not an achievement?"

"That's not what I meant."

"So what did you mean?"

"Whether life has anything in store for you," I say severely.

"Lebert—I'm sixteen. Not three hundred and four: there's lots in store for me. Do you see that room over there that says MALEN SABEL, ANNA MÄRZ, AND MARIE HANGERL?"

"Yes."

"That's what's in store for me next! And tomorrow there'll be something else. Like French, for example. Or math. That's youth."

"Youth is shit," says Glob. "There's far too little time. You're always supposed to be doing something. Why?"

"Because otherwise you'd leave it till tomorrow," says Skinny Felix. "But you can't leave whatever it is till tomorrow. While you're putting it off, your life goes by."

"Where does it say that?" asks Florian.

"In books, I think," says Skinny Felix.

"In books? I thought what was in books was stuff like when the Second World War happened. Or the difference between a main clause and a subordinate clause."

"That's all in books," says Skinny Felix. "But some books just tell you what life is like."

"And what's life like?" says Glob.

"Profound."

Everyone grins.

"Are we profound too?" asks Janosch.

"Don't know. I think right now we're in a phase where we're still looking for the thread. Once we've found it, we're profound too."

"I don't get it." Florian is scandalized. "So what are we before we're profound?"

"I think we're seekers of the thread. That's what youth is—one big thread hunt."

"Youth's still shit," says Janosch.

"Though—I think I'd rather be a thread seeker than profound. Life's too complicated."

"Yes," says Florian, "but girls are hot."

"True." Janosch interrupts him. "Girls are hot. But somehow they're even more complicated than life is."

"Aren't girls what life is?" asks Glob.

"They're certainly part of it," says Florian.

"Which part?" asks Glob.

"The part from the neck to the navel," is Florian's reply.

"Is life female?" asks Skinny Felix.

Janosch grabs a couple of beer cans out of Troy's pajama top. He wants to give them to the girls as soon as he comes into the room, to make clear what a hellish job it was to get the beer upstairs. Janosch thinks Malen goes for guys who pull off difficult stunts. She finds it sexy. I can't be her servant that way. Nor, any longer, can Troy. He puts all the cans down on the parquet floor. It's dark brown and made up of plate-sized rectangles, and you hear every step. But the tutor lives at the other end of the corridor. It's Florian's view that she won't hear us. Janosch knocks on the door. The knock echoes softly, and the sound almost dies away in the large corridor. The girls' hall is bigger than Tarts' Alley. There are sixteen rooms, one right next to the other in a single row. Glob thinks the tutors must have real trouble checking here. Too many rooms. And they're too big. Cupboards and niches provide excellent hiding spots. Even a thousand of them would have a tough time. Janosch knocks again, louder this time. A hushed voice sounds from inside. Unmistakably Malen. "We're waiting. Come in!"

Janosch laughs. His eyes glitter as he swallows a slug of beer. Fat Felix gives him a nudge with his shoulder. They exchange glances for a moment. Janosch puts an encouraging arm around him, then he goes into the room. The others shoot in after him. They're excited. Even Troy doesn't hesitate to get in there. But I wait in the corridor, shifting slowly from my right foot to my left. I stare at the walls. They're white. Unbelievably white. Lots of pictures on them, in large square glass frames. They're photos of the highs and lows of five years of boarding school, at least that's how I read them. Pictures of good times and bad. Maybe a dozen of them. Malen taking a jump on a snowboard. Her long blond hair flies in the wind. She's smiling in a forced sort of way. I wonder if she's really happy, if anyone in boarding school is happy. Janosch says nobody's happy here. Everyone's from some rough family situation. Or else they're stinking rich. And if they are, they're even unhappier. They all have to be laughing in the school brochure, according to him. That's how it always is. They have to be laughing, so that more unhappy kids will be there to laugh in future brochures. That's boarding school. Has been for centuries.

"Doesn't the new guy want to come in with us?" The voice echoes out of the room into the hall. I get ready to go in. I don't want them to get mad or whatever. Besides which I don't want them yelling out into the hall again. If they keep on, there'll be trouble.

"Of course he does." That's Janosch's voice. "He's been thinking about it all night. He even wanted to go up the ladder. Didn't matter what we said."

I go into the room. It's about twice the size of mine. Three beds in this one, spread out all over the place. There's even a small stove. Parquet on the floor, just like in the hall, but a little paler. The same plate-sized rectangles. Three windows. Must be incredibly light during the day. A wooden desk in front of each one. All three the same color as the parquet. Same with the three big cupboards next to the desks. Posters on the walls, too many to count. All of them are either some muscle man licking a

babe out of her bra, or they're Leonardo DiCaprio.
I hate Leonardo DiCaprio. Not that he can help
it. All women love him. Enough already. You have
to be a man to get jealous over stuff like that. It's
obvious.

Chapter 6

The others make themselves comfortable on the floor. The girls have spread out a blue blanket for the occasion. It looks good against the parquet. They're all sitting on it—both Felixes, Janosch, Troy, and Florian. Malen, Anna, and this Marie girl are beside them. They've all had a few already— there are at least three empty wine bottles rolling around on the floor, plus a half bottle of Bacardi O. Now they've switched to beer. Malen's on to her second. Janosch thinks girls in general drink a lot. Supposedly there are regular binges on the girls' corridor. They like it. I have to admit I don't drink much at all—I always have the feeling I'll lose something that maybe I could use. Like my brain. No idea why. But now I'm drinking. Marie invites me to sit down. Next thing there's a beer in my hand. I look at her. She has a round face. Lethal green eyes. Skin a little tanned. Her long dark brown hair is pinned up. Full lips. She's painted them blood red in honor of the event. Or perhaps that's the wine. White teeth, not a single mark on them anywhere. She's mascaraed her eyelashes. Used eye shadow too. She's very slim; she almost disappears inside her black nightshirt. Big breasts, as far as I can make out. The nightshirt doesn't give away much. But I'll get back to them later.

"D'you like it here?" she asks.

"How did *you* like it on your second day?"

"This *is* my second day," she says.

I swallow. "And so how d'you like it now?"

"Now," she says. "The alcohol tastes the same." She laughs, turning her head away. I see her neck. There's a big hickey on it. Pretty quick for your second day. I take a slug of beer.

"What's your name?" she whispers.

"Benjamin."

"Benjamin, like that politician?"

"Yes, Benjamin like that politician."

"Nice name," she says, and swallows some beer. The can's almost empty. She drinks it down, then squashes the can in one tanned hand. It crackles. I notice her fingernails—they're painted red.

"I didn't choose it myself," I say.

"I know, but almost every name marks the person who has it." She stands up. "Will nobody pass me another beer?"

She moves slowly toward her desk. A little unsteady on her feet, but she has a nice walk. I think she's beautiful. She gropes around in a drawer and pulls out some candles. Red, at least a couple of inches long. I look over at Malen, sitting by Janosch.

Crazy

He must be happy. There are two cans of beer lying on the floor. Janosch keeps inching closer to Malen. She's wearing a white silk top and matching panties. Her beautiful legs slide gently away from him across the floor. Janosch wishes he could touch them. I can't blame him. Malen is really stunning. She's powdered her face. Her dark blue eyes blaze out like lasers. You're immediately trapped. Her fingernails and toenails are painted turquoise and seem to give off a strange light. Like Marie, she's pinned her hair up. Her neck is bare. You can see her bra through her silk top. Janosch still doesn't trust himself to touch her legs—his right hand keeps making restless little movements about half an inch above them. He's obviously nervous. Glob says Janosch is often nervous when it comes to girls, almost paralyzed, to the point where he can only play the gentleman. But he's not so good at that. He's just nervous. Not cool like before. And certainly not crazy.

I listen in on their conversation a little. It's more of a squawking match. They're both pretty loaded. I wonder how on earth we'll ever get down the fire escape again. I have another slug of beer. That's one can gone. It's good stuff. Spreads out through my brain. I'm not usually a drinker. That's why I feel it. I start following the conversation again. It's about great sexual disasters. Straight from the talk shows. Malen's in the midst of saying, "The guy had a hard-on. Huge, I'm telling you. And after about an hour he still couldn't get my bra undone. Pathetic, no?"

"Pathetic," says Janosch. "That kind of thing never happens to me." He stares at Malen's tits. She doesn't notice, thank God. All of a sudden the light goes out. Marie is back. She's holding the candles to illuminate the room. The flames dance around the wicks. It looks pretty. Makes me think of my mother. She's always had candles, no matter where we were. Sometimes in the evenings she'd be studying her homeopathic medicine stuff. She'd sit at the dining room table and light a candle. It would be the only light in the house. Not even the television was on, just one candle. And it gave a beautiful light. Has she lit one again tonight? Probably. But then again maybe she didn't have time. Perhaps they had a fight. I don't know. I open another can of beer. Hard to believe there are so many. How on earth did Troy lug them all up here? Fat Felix must have helped. You probably can't see the cans under his potbelly.

Fat Felix is sitting with Anna. They make a great group with Florian and Skinny Felix. Each of them is about to put his arm around Anna. She looks sensational again today. Like Malen she's wearing panties. Hers are black, and they get stuck between the cheeks of her behind. When she bends over to one side, you can see her great ass. I could die. Hard to believe how quickly you can be swept away. Just have to see an ass. Janosch says that's youth for you. Girls just flaunt it. That's it. *Basta.* Sometimes I wonder if things couldn't have been organized differently. When you're barely thirteen, girls and asses become a drug. You never shake the habit. Florian and Fat Felix are good examples—they look like they're devouring Anna. I'm no better. Marie has come to sit next to me again. I can't stop myself from staring down the front of her top.

I drink some more beer. It makes everything simpler. Then I look over at Anna. She's wearing a black T-shirt that says LOVE IS A RAZOR in fancy yellow letters. Maybe it's a real sentence. Then again, maybe it's just crap. *Love* isn't a *razor* or anything else either. Love is indefinable. Love is—fucking is what Janosch would say now. But I don't agree. I think love is more than that. Fucking is fucking. Love is something else. Music maybe. But music is the best. Or at least that's what Frank Zappa said. I think I must be drunk. How did music get in here? Oh yes, Malen put on a CD. The Rolling Stones, of course. *I can't get no satisfaction.* Malen comes back over to Janosch in her panties and her long legs. She sits down. I take another pull at the beer. I'm beginning to like the stuff. Makes you feel good; I don't know why. I immediately drink some more. Marie bends over me. It feels nice. She wants to get some potato chips. Florian thinks chips and alcohol are a deadly combination. They immediately make you throw up, according to him. I still let Marie eat the chips. I picture her bent over the toilet bowl. I have to laugh. Another slug of beer. The can's empty. Funny, I just opened it. Oh well—as I've said before, I'm not used to drinking. Probably why I'm also not used to how quickly the cans get empty. I get a couple more. They're the last two. I take the second one for later and set it down next to me on the floor. Then I cover it with a Kleenex. I don't want anyone else drinking my beer; it's too good for that. Janosch is looking around. He's certainly had a lot to drink. He wants more. You can tell. There's a lit cigarette in the corner of his mouth. It's a large room and the window's open. Nobody's going to smell the smoke that fast. I get out my own cigarettes. The pack's still almost full. Marie wants one too. We both light up on her match, then Marie shakes it and the flame goes out. She puts her arm around me. The speakers are pumping ABBA— "The Winner Takes It All." Good song. Somehow I find it funny. Yet it's actually fairly sad—about people breaking up yet again. I feel pursued. I should call home. Just to make sure they're not beating each other over the head. But not right now. It's nighttime. And besides, Marie's so close. She's almost on top of me. I smell her skin. And a wonderful perfume. Sort of sweet. A little bit like Christmas. Like the Christmas tree or Christmas cookies. Makes me think of last Christmas. They were all there, even my uncle. I love my uncle, but they all spend their time bad-mouthing him. Whenever he's needed, he's not there. Well, he was always there for me. Including Christmas. He works for one of those big daily newspapers. The long articles on page 3 are usually by him. Sometimes he takes me along when he goes to the office. I like it. All the people work behind big tables. They have to tell people about the world. I couldn't do it. I can't even produce a proper piece of homework for school. Last Christmas we had just decided on boarding school and Castle Neuseelen, which was my bad luck, because I was given all sorts of things that would be good for boarding school and Castle Neuseelen. A poster of the local countryside, stuff for all sorts of occasions, a shaving kit, etc. And labels. So that I could stick them all over everything and write my name on them. Benjamin Lebert. Man, I was scared about coming here. And man, I'm still scared now that I've got here. Two days already. Two days and one and a half nights. And now here I am in some girls' dorm room, and there's a girl lying on top of me. Maybe it's progress. She's tickling my neck. Feels strange. I hardly know her. But nice. Janosch says girls in boarding schools are always really up front, particularly the new girls. If I were just a little different, things would happen. What does Janosch mean by *different*? I'm always the same way. Or am I always different? Why is this girl lying on me? Because she's drunk? Because I'm drunk? Doesn't matter. Main thing is she's lying on me. I have another mouthful of beer. I'm getting myself ready to say something, but Marie gets there first. I forget what it was I wanted.

"They told me you were so unusual."

"Unusual? Okay. I'm a cripple. That's pretty unusual."

I take a drag on my cigarette. So does Marie. Her full lips pucker. Sexy. I take another mouthful of beer. Can's empty. I open the next one. Marie gets up—she wants more chips. I look at her body in the flickering light of the candles. It's not long before she lies down with me again. Through her top, I can feel her nipples on my stomach.

"Someone once told me cripples are just people too," she says.

"Funny how much people seem to tell you. Nobody's ever told me anything. I have to find it all out for myself. But okay, you're right, cripples are just people too. Rather odd people." Now it's Guns n' Roses from the speakers, singing "Knockin' on Heaven's Door." I'm not in the mood for songs like this, but still, it's a great song. The old Bob Dylan lyrics haven't lost anything. There's a funny feeling inside me. I swallow more beer.

"So how are you a cripple?" Marie wants to know.

"My left side is almost paralyzed." Marie sighs. "I can hardly move my arm or my leg. They feel numb.

I only feel something if someone actually hurts me." Marie's face moves till it's right next to mine. Our lips are almost touching.

"I won't hurt you," she whispers. "Never. Nor should anyone, ever. It's only people who are completely different who can nourish the growth of something new."

"How old are you?"

"Sixteen," she says.

"That sounds awfully mature for sixteen."

"I know. I'm mature." She grins.

"And what do you think is going to grow out of me?"

"No idea. You'll have to see for yourself. If you're lucky!" And she starts grinning again.

I look over at Troy. He's sitting at the desk. Lonely, all on his own. He must have drunk quite a bit by now. Which is what he always does, according to Fat Felix. Sometimes five or ten beers in an evening. Janosch thinks his stomach can't take it, and at some point Troy always throws up. But he doesn't care. Just starts drinking again. Goes on till morning. Hard as iron. Fat Felix is lying right next to him on the floor. Asleep already, arms and legs sprawled wide, mouth open. He's snoring a little and drooling on the floor. Skinny Felix thinks he started droning on again about soccer, and Janosch filled him up. Now he's out for the count, peaceful as a baby.

I stand up. I've got to get to the john, and quick.

Carefully I ease Marie away from my body. She's settled herself on my legs meantime. I head for the
door. Everything's spinning a little. Never happened
to me before. With an effort I get to the door handle,
push it down, leave the room. Nobody notices—
they're all half out of it already. Only Marie looks
up for a moment. I go down the girls' corridor. It
seems to stretch away forever; it takes me five minutes to reach the john. I open the door. The washroom is markedly nicer and more modern than the
one in Tarts' Alley. There's a big anteroom in front
of me. Everything white tiled. Maybe six washbasins
against the wall. A mirror above each one. I look at
myself. My face looks terrible. I go to one of the
washbasins and splash some water into my face. It
feels good. Refreshing. Suddenly the door opens
behind me with a creak. Marie is in the anteroom.
Wobbling a little. She stands there looking tired.

"What are you doing?"

"Splashing water on my face."

"It's cold?"

"Very."

"Somehow I think we missed out on something,"
she says. Her words are so slurred it's hard to understand her. She pulls her nightshirt over her head.
Now all she's wearing is her black underwear. It
looks wonderful. I see her soft skin. Her navel. Her
face. Her breasts. All a little hazily. She wants something from me. I know that. She comes over to me.

I'm afraid. She touches my neck. I pull away from her several times. I'm shivering. I've never done it with a girl. Girls don't want me. I'm too different. Besides, I'm drunk. No, Marie's drunk. She unhooks her bra. I almost faint. She's standing there in front of me bare to the waist. I see her breasts. They're well shaped, beautiful. Pink nipples. I think of Janosch, who would certainly be saying don't shit in your pants. Use your opportunities. And most of all, grab it. Grab everything you can. I know him. And his advice. According to which I should just lay her. *To lay* is Janosch's best term for *to screw*. Anyone can screw, according to him, but not everyone knows how to lay. That's an art. I'm supposed to lay Marie. Or screw her. Or whatever. If I'm not so scared I shit myself, that is. I wouldn't know—I have no experience.

What if I do something wrong? *So what* is what Janosch says. When you're sixteen, you have to screw. And it's a scandal that I haven't yet. When guys are sixteen that's what they want to do. And when they're sixteen, girls just want to get laid. So we should screw them, in Janosch's view. Marie clearly shares that view, as she's pulling down her panties. I see her pubic hair. It's black. The whole thing looks like a window—it's wide, and trimmed all short. I've never seen anything like it so up close before: in fact I only know what it looks like from *Playboy*. Why does youth have to be so brutal?

Screw here screw there. I'm afraid. Everything's
moving so fast, and I can't keep up somehow. I sit
down on a folding chair by the window. God knows
what it's doing here. Maybe to act as a support in
situations like this? I have no idea. I lean back as far
as I can go. Marie takes another step toward me. Her
large breasts are almost in my face. She bends over
me a little, strokes her fingers gently across my hips.
As she does so, her upper body moves. Her tits
swing. I get a hard-on. That must be how it happens,
I think. It's natural. But I still feel like an idiot. I pull
my pajama top down over the pants and hold my
hands over it. My forehead's sweating. It's still the
same old pair of pajamas—*When the going gets
tough, the tough get going.* I find myself thinking
about my father. Marie kisses my forehead. I start to
shake. Turn away. Shit, I say to myself, so I'll screw
her. Gotta be a man, as Janosch would put it. And a
man doesn't panic at the sight of a pair of tits. A man
should grab. Handle them. A man should be cool,
per Janosch. Unfortunately he can't help right now.
I'm on my own. Got to do it somehow, or at least
try. I pull my pajama pants down a ways. Marie can
see my cock. She scrabbles around and pulls a condom out of the stuff lying on the floor. Opens the
packet with her teeth. Rolls on the condom. It's
done in a flash. Feels funny. So tight. So rubbery.
Like a wet balloon. But stickier. I'm nervous. The
condom's yellow. I wonder how she found it so

quickly. Janosch says they all do. They can always hunt up a condom, so that they can fuck right away. Marie sits herself astride me. I think I'm inside her. It doesn't feel good. Screwing isn't as great as they all say. I feel all boxed in. My cock hurts. But I'm a man. I grab for her tits. I squeeze them together. Lick her nipples. Her tits are soft. They feel so good lying in my hands. I'm not going to forget this in a hurry. Florian says you never forget your first pair of tits; they're the best. I guess he's right. Marie grinds harder with her pelvis. My cock keeps getting bigger. She moans. Sweats a little. *She's* the one doing all the work. I'm just sitting here. But I'm beginning to like it. I feel good, sort of like I'd drunk twenty Cokes or something. My whole body's tingling. Most of all my cock. The tingling makes me push up farther. I lean forward, and grab Marie by the hips. Put my arms right around her. Squeeze her ass. We cuddle tight. She moans. I'm breathing harder. Marie rides and rides. We're almost there. My cock's being pushed out and in again. The first time's like this, says Janosch. A quick knock. A quick glance inside. A quick goodbye. Marie keeps riding me. Sweat forms on her skin and I lick it off. Put my head between her tits. She doesn't say a word. The whole time. Just moans. Suddenly she throws her arms up in the air. I'm going to come. Maybe another five seconds, and I'm there. I ejaculate. Adrenaline shoots through my body. I feel free. I can hear birds. Water running. A whole storm. My body's shaking. It's the coolest thing ever. I don't know why, but it's crazy. And I want it again soon.

Marie comes too. At least I think she does. She moans louder than before. Holds her own tits. Gives one loud cry, then crumples. We cuddle. That certainly wasn't her first time; I'm sure of it. She's far too good at it. Janosch thinks doing it the first time with an experienced girl is good. You don't have to do so much, because she knows what to do already. Marie dismounts, stumbles across the anteroom. Doesn't say a word. Pulls her panties back on. I see her cunt again for a moment. I'll remember it for sure. So that was my first time. And in Neuseelen Boarding School. And on my second night. It all went pretty fast. I start to feel bad. Really rotten. As if someone had kicked me in the balls. I can hardly stand and my knees are shaking. The beer rumbles in my stomach. All shaken up by the quickie with Marie. My head hurts and my eyes are watering. Marie leaves. I watch her stumble out the door. She must be pretty drunk, I think. I'm not even sure she knew what she was doing. Maybe she does this a lot. Doesn't care what happens next. Maybe just wants to have fun and doesn't give a shit. Okay, so what. What are all those sayings about your first time? After your first time you're a man? Now you're really standing on your own feet? Farewell to sweet youth? Now you're a grown-up? My first time's over now, and I still feel small enough to piss in my pants. Which is okay too. I don't want to become a grown-up; I want to remain a perfectly normal kid. Have fun. Hide behind my parents when I have to. And all that's over now? Just because I put my cock in Marie's hot little hole? But nobody saw. And I'm not going to tell anyone.

The good Lord should cut me some slack. We can behave as if nothing happened. The whole thing is beginning to get too complicated for me. Why do I ever have to grow up? Or to put it another way, what moron ever came up with this idea in the first place? Why don't we all just stay small boys? Who want to have fun? Screw, laugh, be happy. I pace around the anteroom. I'm upset. As if a dream has died or something. As if something is over. I'm still shaking. My skin's gone white. I feel alone. In the whole damn wide world. In this shitty boarding school. And it would have to be called Neuseelen — "New Souls." My soul is new, all right. That's for sure. My shitty soul. I miss home. My parents. Why do they fight? Where's my sister? And why the hell am I turning so aggressive? I've just screwed a girl, goddamnit. One who was drunk. With big tits and a hot cunt. And who apparently didn't even notice. Stroke of luck, huh? I splash some water on my face. Then I go to take a piss. I've been needing a piss for a long time. I think I may have wet my pants a little already. I'm still wearing this disgusting condom. It's hanging down slack. My cock's not hard enough anymore. I chuck it on the floor. It can be their problem tomorrow, if the cleaning woman finds it. If whoever finds it. I step to the edge of the toilet. Lift the seat. Piss. Piss off to the side as well. I don't care. For a moment I even piss deliberately against the wall. The way they always do in Tarts' Alley. It's great. It all runs over the floor. Almost a flood. I get a real laugh out of it. Then I go down on my knees. Throw up. And keep throwing up.

Today was a bit too much for me: instead of a night in bed, climbing a fire escape, drinking everything in sight, screwing around a little, and growing up along the way. Enough for one night. Enough to make anyone puke. I stand up and stagger out into the anteroom. There are a couple of stains on my pajama top. So what. The yellow condom's lying on the tile floor. The white stuff's collecting in the tip. You can see it clearly. Someone's going to get a kick out of that tomorrow. Maybe Malen. Maybe one of the tutors. I go out into the girls' corridor. Look at all the pictures on the wall. Look at Malen's picture and the pictures of the others. Listen to the sound of my footsteps. I'm on my own. Nobody's giving me a hand. I stand outside room 330. Malen's room. A normal door made of gray plywood, with a normal brass handle. I push it down.

Chapter 7

How do you describe life in boarding school? As difficult? Boring? Demanding? Lonely would be another. I feel lonely. Even though I'm with the others all day long. Let's take a perfectly ordinary day: I wake up at six-thirty. Landorf, the teacher in charge, is standing in the doorway.

"It's time," he says.

Slowly I raise my head. Look over at Janosch. All I can see is his mess of hair. We still have another half hour. Janosch chooses to use his for sleep. He never washes in the morning. I get up. Take my shaving kit. Shuffle down Tarts' Alley. Breakfast at seven-fifteen. Rolls, Nutella, yogurt. Classes begin at seven forty-five. First comes learning. You just sit there for half an hour and learn. They call it Silentium. Only in boarding school. Usually you hold up a book in front of you and nod off. Sometimes it falls over. Embarrassing. Then classes start. Six hours a day, Saturdays included. A long break after the second, a short one after the fourth. You go get sandwiches from the case outside the dining hall. They taste disgusting.

One-fifteen lunch. The menu's posted at the entrance to the dining hall. Usually rice with some kind of sauce. Every six weeks you have to wait tables. While the others eat, you get to run around. Set and clear the tables. When everything's over, it's your turn. You eat with the staff in the kitchen. After lunch you're free for an hour. Afternoons: doing homework. Then supper. Two hours free. Then washroom. Then sleep. Bedtime for sixteen-year-olds is ten-thirty.

How can you describe life in boarding school?

I've been here four months.

I go into Troy's room. There's a little light coming through the open window. The curtains are moving in the wind, their shadows dancing on the cracked parquet floor. The floor is gray and radiates depression. There are a couple of posters on the pock-marked wall. They all show scenes of horror from the Second World War. Screaming children. Bombed-out cities. Desperate soldiers. Next to them are some newspaper articles about the SS. I see hideous faces. Goebbels. Göring. Hitler. There's a sentence written on the wall in a color that looks like blood: IS THIS THE WAY LIFE'S MEANT TO BE? The letters run into each other, but you can make them out. Only one bed in here, placed in the middle of the room. The pillows are tangled up in the bedcover, but you can see it has a scene from the movie *Dragonheart* on it, with a huge fire-belching dragon fighting one of the knights of the Round Table. WE WILL ALWAYS SUCCEED is written on it. The desk is to the right, next to the window, heaped with stuff, mainly books, colored pens, and photos. Some drawings are stacked on the windowsill. Naked women with big breasts. I've never been here before. Somehow I'm ashamed about this. I take another step into the room. There's a storage cupboard against the left wall. Full of books. Troy himself is in front of it in the act of pulling one out. Stephen King's *Misery*. It's a great book. I know it. It's about this novelist who has a car accident. He finally ends up with a madwoman who tortures him. Cuts off one of his legs and so on. She says she's his greatest fan, and he has to write a book for her. If he doesn't, he'll die. It's that simple. Terrific book. At my last school, I suggested it for our German reading class. That got me a 6. We read *Soul Flame*. Piece of shit. I didn't understand a word. As far as I remember, the only books we read in school were ones I didn't understand. The authors always seem to talk in riddles; they could actually be writing a quiz book or something. Probably I just don't get it. Still. I go over to Troy. Sit down by him on the bed. On the edge, of course, I don't want to bug him. He frowns irritably. He holds up *Misery*. It has a green binding with silver lettering, which truly sparkles when you get it in the right light. The guy's really made it, I think to myself. No more problems. Stephen King has millions and millions in the bank. He doesn't care whether his son gets a 6 in math or not. Keeps on living. Writes his books and is happy. Stephen King can kiss my ass. I've handed in another two pieces of homework in the last week. I think they're both lousy. I haven't got them back yet. Math and German. Everything seems to be getting on my nerves right now.

The bed I'm sitting on is incredibly soft. What I'd really like to do right now is go to sleep. I could also use it. We were out again last night. Down in front of the dining hall. A little smoking, a little talking. Just enjoying ourselves. Janosch says we should do it more often. But I don't know if that's such a good idea. Everyone needs a little sleep, too, in my view. I look around. The room is really small. Does Troy like it in here? I have no idea. I lean back. Look at the clock. Five-thirty. Another hour until supper.

"Troy, what are you doing?"

"Nothing."

"But you have to be doing something!"

"No I don't."

I turn my head a little to the right. Run a hand over my hair. Troy remains sitting next to me. A fly crawls over his face. He doesn't try to shoo it away. Stays still. His eyes roll. He coughs a little.

Crazy

"Why are you alone, Troy?" I try again. "Why do you want to be alone?"

Troy's eyes are somewhere far away. He's struggling with himself. He doesn't often get questions like this. And he doesn't often have to answer them. He clears his throat.

"I'm different, you know," he says in a deep voice. "Just different. People don't like people who are different. That's how it is. People don't take notice of me. They don't like me." Troy looks up at me, and his eyes flicker. His lips tighten. It's the first time I've heard him say anything like this. His eyes watch me good-naturedly.

"But we like you, Troy!" I say. I rub my left arm. "We like you."

"You register me," Troy replies. "But you don't like me. You only take me with you all the time because you have to. Maybe to carry the beer. Or to beat up on me. Janosch always needs someone to beat up on."

"But you belong with us," I say. "Like Florian or Fat Felix. You're one of us. A hero, as Janosch would say. We wouldn't amount to much without you."

"I'm not a hero. Nobody's ever paid attention to me. I'm a bed wetter. See for yourself!"

He slowly pulls the *Dragonheart* bedcover aside. There's a big stain on the sheet.

"It happens to me at night," he says. "I piss in the bed. I don't know why. Nobody would understand.

So I prefer being alone. If you're alone, nobody can hurt you."

Troy stands up, goes over to the window, stands there a minute. Then comes back to the bed, sits down.

"Are you ever afraid?" he asks. "I don't mean afraid of an exam. Or a teacher. Just plain afraid—afraid of life, you know?" Troy swallows. He hunches forward.

"Life *is* being afraid," I say. I'm beginning to feel uncomfortable. In truth, I've never thought about it. But I think it's true. "That's how it has to be," I say. "I don't know why either, but somehow that's the way it has to be! Maybe because otherwise people would spend their time behaving like idiots. They wouldn't be afraid anymore."

"But does that mean it has to be that way all the time?" asks Troy. "I don't want to be afraid all the time. Everything always happens so fast. I can't keep up. I'm afraid."

"You're right, Troy. It all happens too fast. Why can't we wait? Just look. Rewind?"

"Because life isn't really a videotape?" Troy says timidly. "So what is it?"

Troy's getting nervous. He rubs his eyes. The sweat's beginning to build on his forehead. He takes a deep breath. "Life is . . ." He falters. Shivers. He's rocking backward and forward from the waist. The fly abandons his face, looking for somewhere quieter. The chair. The table. It keeps crawling.

"It's . . . ?" I repeat.

"It's a big wet bed," he finally bursts out.

He's crying. Fat tears roll down his face. His eyes start to swell. He sobs. I move closer to him. I didn't mean this to happen. Cautiously I stroke his back with my right hand.

"God's no use," Troy stutters. "He doesn't lift a finger. He just sits up there fat and happy and does nothing to help." He puts his hands over his face. Doubles up. Cries. You can hear his silent lament.

"He'll help us at some point, Troy," I say. "At some point. Someday he'll come and get us out of this shit down here and help us, Troy. You and me. The two of us will laugh when all this is over, and life stops being one big wet bed!"

"Life will always be one big wet bed," he says despairingly. His skin is all damp and his cheeks are wet with tears. "I can't go on, Lebert!" he says. "I can't. Where the hell are we going?"

He's at the end of his rope; you can tell. At some point everyone reaches the end of their rope. Even silent Troy. Janosch calls it the "Tart House phase." When nothing makes sense. When you've had enough. Then you break down, according to him. He says it's perfectly okay; that if you don't, you'll die.

I don't know if it's good or not. What I think is that you only bitch about the stuff you have no right

to bitch about. But I haven't a clue. I would certainly never have expected it from Troy—I always
thought he just *was*. Like the moon or the stars.
He would never have a Tart House phase. But
that's where you go wrong. Youth's a bummer, says
Janosch. Everyone has problems. Even Troy. He's
blowing his nose right now. I keep stroking his back.

I find myself thinking about my parents. About
the weekends we've spent together recently. Everything seemed so hard somehow. I never felt completely relaxed. There was always the feeling that I'd
have to return to school soon. Everything we did felt
bad. I was pissed off. At myself. At my father and
mother. At my sister. At the fact that everything has
to be over sometime. And that I should be leading
my own life someplace else—in school, in fact.
Janosch says that's the tragedy of being at boarding
school. Every Sunday you have to go back. That's it.
Basta. Always cheerful and in the old communal
frame of mind—one for all, etc.

Pretty exhausting, in his view. Being at home is a
lot nicer. I think he's right. Even if my parents fight
a lot. Almost every weekend when I've been home,
my mother cries. She sits in the kitchen with tears
running down her cheeks. Just like Troy. While my
sister sits beside her to comfort her. Both of them
furious with my father. I was always in the middle.
Didn't want to attack either one of them. I felt we
were all somehow at fault. It's all so complicated.

Crazy

Too complicated for me, anyway. I don't get it. If I didn't know better, I'd say what I needed was a Tart House phase. Scream the whole thing out for once, to clear everything up. It hurts to see your mother cry. Sometimes that's the last image I have of her as I leave again for Neuseelen. Crying—in the kitchen, on the red stool, in front of the window. There's a saying that youth is easy. People who say it are the ones who've already got it behind them—they must be wishing they had it back. I don't think it's such a good idea. God, everything's miserable. Troy can do a real number on that. I have no idea how I should comfort him. I can hardly tell him he should just stop pissing in his bed, but I'd like to help him. I'm sorry for him. He's never had any luck at all in his life.

"Let's get out," he says. "Just run. Let's get the others and disappear. Who cares where. It's a big world. I can't stand it here any longer."

"We can't. They'll look for us and they'll find us. The world's smaller than you think. At least the boarding-school world. We can't clear out. It's too dangerous."

"If we're quick, we can do it," says Troy. "We can go to Munich. Before supper. There's a bus to Rosenheim. Then we can go on by train." Troy tries to make eye contact with me. He looks at me with blank sadness. The guy really means it—you can tell.

"Please don't make me an onlooker anymore," he says. "Don't leave me standing in the dark, staring at the stage. My whole life I've been staring at the stage. I've had it. Now I want to be up on the stage. Do something wild. Something no one's ever done before. Something *crazy*."

"*Crazy?*"

"*Crazy.*"

I don't say anything. I'm not really all that thrilled with this. I don't want to clear out. Things will certainly turn unpleasant. And where are we supposed to spend the night? Neuseelen closes its gates at 11:00 p.m. After that nobody can get in or out. All the better, Janosch would say; then we'll just spend the night in Munich. The only question is where. The people at school are certain to miss us pretty soon. There'll be an uproar. I lean back slowly and take a deep breath.

"Has anyone done this before?" I ask.

"What?"

"You know, take an illegal trip to Munich and spend the night. Just like that. Without saying we're going."

"Not since I've been here," answers Troy. "And certainly no one our age. You just can't let yourself do things like that. It's semicriminal." He laughs.

"But then why are we going to let ourselves do it?"

"Because we're the best. Think for a minute.

Crazy

Who better than the six of us to act out the wildest idea of all time? Janosch, the two Felixes, Florian, you, and me. We were born for wild ideas." Troy laughs. His eyes are sparkling. I don't think he's ever been so happy before. He's beside himself, rocking backward and forward, the tears at the corners of his eyes drying, leaving little red marks.

Silent Troy has jumped over his own shadow. You can tell. He's on the road to recovery. His mouth is still dark and twisted, but he's smiling. He stands up.

"The six of us."

Chapter 8

"You want to split?" asks Janosch, enraptured, when I pull him out of our room. I have just packed the most important things into my blue backpack. Water. A few bars of chocolate. A book. You never know; maybe I'll take to reading. Could be. Janosch grins. There's the light of adventure in his eyes. He's quite excited, as far as I can tell.

Florian says that for Janosch, this is the greatest. He always wanted to run away but never trusted himself to manage it on his own. Now he's got a whole mob behind him. So he's got to join in—he's too crazy not to, according to Florian. Florian a.k.a. Girl is also in. He thinks it's too boring here anyway. And he's got Skinny Felix onboard. He wasn't too keen at the beginning—too dangerous—but now he's with us. It's how it has to be. The whole thing is too exciting to let it just roll on by. The same goes for Fat Felix. He took a nap for a couple of hours this afternoon, so he has no idea yet how lucky he is. Janosch wants to wake him. We don't think this is such a good idea.

"You're too rough," says Skinny Felix.

"Me, too rough?" asks Janosch. "Come on—Glob loves me! The idea of taking an illegal trip to Munich with me will thrill him, for sure. I know him." Janosch goes into Glob's room. Less than two minutes later he comes back out, towing Fat Felix.

Felix looks half asleep. His eyes are tiny, and his hair is down over his face. He looks a sight. We all laugh. You can still see the creases from the pillows on his cheeks. He starts waving his arms wildly.

"You guys are nuts!"

"Of course we're nuts," says Janosch. "That's why we need someone who isn't. And since Mr. Teacher Landorf won't be coming, we immediately thought of you!"

"You're right," says Felix. "But because I'm not nuts, I'm not coming."

"That's what we thought," says Janosch, "but we need you. You have to come too! Most people need a port in a storm. You're our storm in a port."

"Your storm in a port?"

"Yes, our big sugar treat," Janosch explains.

"And what exactly makes me your big sugar treat?" Felix wants to know.

"Because Malen isn't coming," answers Janosch. "That's what makes you our big sugar treat. But I think you're up to it. Your tits are just as big." Janosch puts his arm around Fat Felix.

"Can I take a backpack with some candy?" he asks. "I can't help it—I need it."

"Take whatever you want," is Janosch's reply, "but please, no roast pork or anything like that. Now move!"

"You've just given me a great idea," Glob interrupts. "Munich must be pork heaven. Do you think I could get some?"

"If the answer's yes, will that make you come?"

"You can bet on it," says Felix.

"You'll come just because there's something to eat!" Janosch is exasperated. "You're too fat as it is."

"Too fat, maybe," says Felix, "but I'm still your storm in a port. You said so."

"Okay, okay," says Janosch. "But get moving! A city like Munich isn't going to wait for us forever."

"Is Munich really cool?" asks Skinny Felix as Glob vanishes back into his room.

"Munich's cool," says Janosch.

"Crazy," adds Florian.

"Does it have women?" asks Skinny Felix.

"Munich has millions of people," Janosch tells him. "It has women the way it has roast pork—on every street corner.

"We're really going to go?"

"Of course we're going. We're men."

"When?"

"In a minute, provided Glob shows up soon."

A big red hiking backpack comes around the corner, packed to the very top. Under the buckle you can make out a bag of candy—it obviously barely made it. Fat Felix closes the door to his room and comes toward us with deliberate strides. My watch says 6:15 p.m.

"Thank God such a giant backpack won't attract attention," Janosch observes as we go racing down the Castle hill. "Who would ever think we'd planned any kind of a long trip, Glob. Well done!"

"Sorry, but you yourself said I can bring whatever I want."

"True," retorts Janosch, "but I never thought of a baby elephant."

Felix says, "Nothing we can do about it now — we're already on our way. Would anyone like a chocolate snail?"

"I'll stick a chocolate snail up your ass," says Janosch.

"Does that mean no?"

"No. A definite no."

At this moment up pipes little Florian a.k.a. Girl. "I don't want to depress you, but where the hell are we going to spend the night tonight?"

"We'll find something," says Janosch. "Munich's a big place. Are any of you afraid, by any chance?"

"I'm not," says Skinny Felix.

"Me neither," says Florian. "Well, maybe just a bit. But it'll go away, right? I mean, it can't get that bad."

"It'll go away," says Janosch. "We're doing okay."

"Go away?" Fat Felix answers him. "It's supposed to go away? It never goes away. For the last two years I've been taking part in shit and I'm still afraid every time. I sometimes wonder why I keep letting myself be talked into things."

"Because you need it," says Janosch. "We all need it. We're young. Even Troy needs it."

"Oh no," says Glob. "I do not need it. And Troy doesn't either, do you, Troy? Do you need it?"

"Yes I do," Troy says, bringing up the rear, marching slowly down the Castle hill. I'm next to him on the tarred road, which is just wide enough for one car, and winds its way laboriously up toward the Castle, surrounded by trees. Everything here is spring green. Looks beautiful. The sun comes slanting down through the treetops, making patterns of light on the ground. Janosch and the others cut across them as they move on ahead. I'm thinking.

How often have I driven up this road in my father's old Renault? How often have I cried? Said I didn't want to stay here, that everything was so awful, and I couldn't go on. My father always got mad. Said I should pull myself together. This was life. He couldn't do anything about it either. Everyone had to go through it, and that was that. Then he dropped me off with my case, a green traveling bag. Two CDs packed into the side pockets. *The Rolling Stones Collection 1* and *2*. My father said they would help. Bring me more energy. Appetite for life. Who knows? I think it's all crap. First I stood in the parking lot at Neuseelen for five minutes and cried. Then I went on up, and into my room. To Janosch. Not that he ever really comforted me; still, he was there. Had a smoke with me. Talked about life. Rendered judgment. Somehow I was glad to see him. Janosch is a rock. Everyone knows that, even Fat Felix, even when he won't admit it. Florian says you need a rock like that in life. Then you never lose your way or need to be afraid. I think he's right. As long as Janosch is there, I'm not afraid. Not that he's particularly big or strong. He's just Janosch. That's enough.

"See, Glob, you need it!" says Janosch, and bursts out laughing. "You need it! You need us! If Troy needs us, you need us too."

"Bullshit," says Fat Felix. "Nobody needs you. Or us. Why are we here anyway? The world wouldn't be any different without us."

"That's not true," Skinny Felix interjects. "There's a reason we're here."

"Which is?" asks Janosch.

"Well, I don't exactly know. Maybe it's so we can observe everything."

"Observe everything?" asks Janosch. "Does that mean we're just spectators? Cheap spectators?"

"We're just observers," is Skinny Felix's reply. "We'll all find our little spots in God's big cemetery. And nobody will even think about us anymore."

"How about getting really gloomy?" says Glob. "Maybe I'll be famous, and when I die, everyone will weep over me like they did with Princess Di."

"That's different," says Janosch. "Princess Di was always Princess Di. And will stay Princess Di forever. People will remember her. Nobody'll remember us. That's life. We're just kids in boarding school. Nobody even thinks about us."

"It's all so frustrating," says Glob. "I mean, we're alive here. We must have created some movement."

"Yeah, we broke out of boarding school," says Florian.

"They're probably looking for us already."

"No—they're still eating," says Janosch.

"Hang on, guys," says Glob. "How come we're able to live without knowing why?"

"Oh—it's quite simple," is Janosch's reply. "We're always doing things without knowing why. Now, for example. Don't shit your pants! Maybe it's a good thing that nobody's worrying about us. Besides, we'll certainly remember."

"Remember what?"

"Ourselves."

"Ourselves?"

"Yes, ourselves," says Janosch. "I hereby resolve to remember you guys, and all the crazy things that've happened to us. That's how we go on living somehow. Don't ask me why, but it's true."

"You're sure?" asks Glob.

"Quite sure. Won't you guys remember?"

"Sure," says Florian a.k.a. Girl.

"Me too," adds Skinny Felix.

"And you, Glob?" asks Janosch.

"I have to think about it. But I think I will."

"The whole thing's been *crazy.*"

"You see!" says Janosch. "That's how we'll go on with our lives. Tell your children and your grandchildren about it. It's not like it'll become some famous story. But we'll go on living."

"Troy as well?" asks Florian.

"Troy as well. We all will. Where's Benni?"

"Here!"

We're making tracks. We've almost reached the village.

Same old tune. The one about the six kids at boarding school. We keep walking downhill. Dusk is falling. I'm afraid, but I don't know why. Probably the night. I never liked it. It hides so many secrets, and it's so empty and bleak. All great views turn black at night. Yet black is my favorite color. But only when it's a light black.

Janosch says if we're lucky we'll still catch the last bus. It'll take us to Rosenheim. Little Bavarian town.

Florian says it's full of extreme right-wingers. He doesn't want to spend any time there. Janosch says it'll be okay. We'll go on again by train right away to Munich. The big city. Where I live, where my parents are. Where they fight. I talked to my sister on the phone recently. She says it's all horrible. They haven't exchanged a single reasonable word between them. Now my father's living in a hotel, the Leopold. She gave me the number: 089/367061. I've never called. He would only talk my head off. About how sorry he is about everything. And that things really won't change for me. It's all crap. Of course things will change for me.

So what's it all about? I look around at my five friends. They're a little preoccupied. You can see the uncertainty in their eyes. Janosch, the ringleader, is walking out in front, looking down at the ground. He's wearing a black polo shirt and white jeans. His blond hair is flopping down into his face. The chain around his neck, which has a medallion hanging on it with a photo of his parents, moves with every step. He never takes the chain off, not even when he goes to bed. Fat Felix says Janosch loves his parents more than anything in the world. Sometimes he even cries after he's been home for a long visit. And there's nothing he wants more than to be with them whenever he can.

Next to him is Florian a.k.a. Girl. He's a bit unsteady on his feet. He keeps looking at nature.

Crazy

He's searching for the light, watching the sun go down. His hair is combed back, and he's wearing a red Adidas training suit. The three stripes cover the whole surface. It looks terrible. Janosch thinks Florian doesn't care how he looks. Main thing is to look like something; he doesn't care. He just puts on his clothes the way anybody does. The only difference is that sometimes he achieves the most god-awful combinations. Once he came to school wearing unmatching socks. He didn't even notice. It's all the same to him. That's what makes it funny, according to Janosch.

Behind him are the two Felixes. They and I are the only ones who've brought backpacks. Glob's is red, Felix's blue. Side by side like that, they look comic. They follow the others in silence, a good fifteen feet behind Janosch and Florian. But it doesn't bother anyone.

They walk on quietly. Glob is wearing a blue woolen sweater and brown corduroys. His eyes are moist. On his head is a red Ferrari cap. Fat Felix loves Ferrari. He has a catalog with all the models in it. At night he even takes it to bed with him and sniffs it. His greatest wish is to drive in a Ferrari just once, top down, etc. But you know he'd scream if it ever actually happened.

Skinny Felix is wearing a green hooded sweatshirt that comes way down over his forehead. His quick, dark eyes glint out from underneath. His feet are in white gym shoes. Skinny Felix is a gym-shoe fanatic. He knows them all. He's got thousands in his cupboard. He wants to create his own line of gym shoes later on. He knows it's nuts, but so what.

Behind the two of them is Troy. He's practically asleep on his feet. His little round eyes are heavy. He's wearing a black waterproof cape, but it's not raining. Troy was given the cape by his brother. He won't live much longer—maybe another couple of months, apparently. Sometimes, when he's a little loaded, Troy talks about him. The brother is called Nicholas or something. He's exactly a year older than Troy. Troy likes him; he's crazy about him. He doesn't want to lose him, which is why when things get exciting he always wears the waterproof cape, to be with his brother and so not to leave him alone. Janosch says it's gallant. I agree. And behind him, and a little to one side, there's me. It's the usual thing. I walk slowly and with difficulty. My left foot drags. I'd like to cut it off. I'm wearing a Pink Floyd T-shirt again. This one's from the album *The Division Bell*. There are two big rocks on it, with eyes and mouths. They look like they're talking to each other. At a distance you'd think there was only one of them. Typical Pink Floyd. I like Pink Floyd. Janosch says their music is *crazy*. But that's why I like it. *We don't need no education* gets right under your skin. They're right, in my opinion. I'm also wearing blue jeans. Levi's. I got them from my sister. She says they work really well for getting girls. She should know what she's talking about, even if I don't. It's great having a gay sister; she always has pretty friends, although they're also mostly gay too. Janosch says it's cool. You just have to convert them to the right sex, or whatever. Janosch thinks all lesbians secretly dream of switching. I'm not sure he's right. In any case a conversion like that is tough. I tried it once.

She was called Manuela or something and was almost twenty. I was just fourteen. And head over heels in love with her. She was about five feet eight inches, with brown shoulder-length hair. Her eyes were like the sea, blue and remote. I don't think I'll forget her anytime soon. Once she even kissed me. In my sister's room, when she wasn't there. We were watching TV. *Die Hard,* or something. And all of a sudden she bent over me. I almost died. Man, she could kiss. But it never turned into anything serious. She said I was too strange. Usual thing. Janosch says he can understand that. He thinks I'm strange too. But in a positive way. *Crazy,* even. He says I'm the craziest person he ever met. Florian thinks I shouldn't let this go to my head—Janosch would say it to anyone. But we get on really well together anyway. After all, we've already spent four months in the same room.

Chapter 9

I see the bus stop off in the distance. Just a sign with a bench in front of it, right on the main road. The sign says BUS STOP NEUSEELEN. The bench is made of dark beechwood. Yesterday's rain is seeping into the cracks. An occasional drip lands on the asphalt. There's an old man sitting at one end of the bench. He's very thin, with a messy thatch of white hair. He's wearing a green raincoat that reaches to his feet. Shiny black galoshes poke out from underneath. The raincoat is held closed by a single button. The old man looks up as we come closer. Janosch is out ahead, with Florian, the two Felixes, and Troy behind. I'm following, in the rear. The others stop at the sign, their faces squashed up against the bus schedule.

"Are you from the Castle?" the old man asks. His voice is deep and resonant. The guys turn around. Glob is the first to find his voice.

"Yes, we have a pass."

The old man's eyes narrow, and there's a pale glint in them. He purses his mouth.

"Don't try to con an old man," he says. "An old

man may be deaf. May be blind. May even be a cripple. But an old man has sung the song of life too often to be conned. You don't have a pass. Am I right? You're running away."

"Running away?" asks Glob.

"The song of life?" asks Janosch. "What the hell is that?"

"The unmistakable facts of human existence," replies the old man. "The ones no one can hide. Grief, joy, wind."

"What's the wind got to do with it?" I ask.

"The wind that mixes grief and joy and, when necessary, tears everything apart or joins it back together. You can call it what you like."

"Are you a wise man or a seer or something?" asks Skinny Felix.

The old man laughs, and his laugh sounds like an oncoming steamroller forcibly clearing a path. The guys look around surreptitiously.

"I'm not a seer," says the old man, "and as far as I know, I'm not a wise man either. I'm just an old man, and I've seen life. That's enough to give me something to say about it."

"Will we get that way too?" asks Glob.

"What way?" says the old man.

"You know—old."

"You will certainly get old, my boy. That's life. All parts of you will get old: your soul, your heart, your opinions. Even if you don't change that quickly, your opinions will. And your dreams. At some point they're just old. Like you!"

"But when they're old, are they still good?" Glob wants to know. "Why do dreams have to get old?"

"To leave life behind," says the man.

"To leave life behind?" Glob repeats. "I don't get it. Does that mean you always have to leave something old behind to get something new?"

"In my view, yes. That way everything remains in motion," says the old man.

"But does that mean it can't ever stand still?" asks Glob. "Why do we have to keep running? We could just as easily stand still. Catch our breath. Look at wherever we've reached in peace."

"No we couldn't," says the old man.

"So why not?" asks Fat Felix.

"Because then everything would have to stand still. For us to look at wherever we've reached in peace, both we and the wherever would have to stand still. And if we stand still, there are no wherevers to be reached. It would just be one big unending standing still. Come on, my boy, tell me honestly: Which would you prefer? To be perpetually standing still or perpetually running?"

"That was the song of life you just sang, wasn't it?" asks Glob. "Does everyone sing it when they get old?"

"That depends," says the old man. "Whether you grow old or not is a matter of chance. And whether you sing the song of life or not is up to God. It's that simple."

"Call that simple?" asks Fat Felix. "It's far too complicated. I don't think I want to get old, and I don't want to sing the song of life either. It's much easier just living in a world you don't understand. I don't want to get old. Getting old is too *crazy*. I'd rather stay myself, Felix Braun, sixteen years old, five foot four, that's it."

"All that's pure chance," says the old man.

"It's not chance," retorts Janosch. "There's no such thing as chance. There's just fate."

"So our meeting here is fate?" asks the old man.

"Maybe," says Janosch. "And maybe it's just bad luck. I'm sixteen years old. Life goes on. And on. And I don't want people who are farther along telling me how the whole thing goes. I had to get through the last sixteen years without you and I'll probably have to get through the next sixty-five years, God willing, without you as well. So just leave me alone. It's great that you can sing the song of life, so go take it to an old-age home and teach it to the residents! They'd be thrilled! But leave me to get on with it. Leave yourself to get on with it too. Everything's bad enough as it is. We've just run away from boarding school. And I think we're going to need what's left of our youth. Go peddle your crappy song someplace else!" Janosch's eyes are slits. He's really mad.

"Is your friend always so rude?" asks the old man.

"He invented the word," says Glob.

"When I was up there in school at Neuseelen, we had one like him. He was the leader of our gang. Xavier Mils. I don't know what happened to him. I think he was a sculptor or something. Long time ago. In Munich. I haven't heard a word from him in fifty years. Maybe he's dead. The way I see it, the only one allowed to be more superfluous is me. But that's the way it is. Life. You said you were running away? Where do you want to spend the night? If you're headed for Munich, I don't see you having much luck. You won't find it easy to get something. But I don't advise you to spend the night on a park bench. Munich is dangerous, particularly at night; you get some strange types roaming around, I can tell you. Maybe it would be best if you stay with me. I own a little apartment in Schwabing. It's not very large, but you could all fit in. At least nothing will happen to you there. You'll be safe. I've been living there for twenty-five years. Alone. And nothing's ever happened to me. The graveyard at Neuseelen, where my wife is, is more dangerous. If I remember right, I even have some spare bedding."

Glob, Florian, and Skinny Felix turn around—

they're thinking. Janosch pulls an angry face and sits down beside me on the bench.

"I don't like the old guy," he whispers. "He's really weird. Something about him is off. I wouldn't want to go to his apartment with him. He's crazy."

"You don't know that," I say. "Maybe he's just an old man who's very open and who wants the best for us. You heard—he was in school at Neuseelen himself. He seems well intentioned. Maybe he knows our problems, and he's some kind of a seer or something."

"He's raving," says Janosch, "and my mother taught me you should never listen to people who're raving. You should get out of their way."

"Then a lot of us would have to get out of your way too," I say. "We're all raving. All he is, is old."

"But that's the point," says Janosch. "He's old and we're young. The two don't go together. They never have. Old people have a completely different attitude to life. They don't like us. And we don't like them. No kid on earth would set off to Munich with this old guy right now. And what's he doing here anyway? He lives in Munich."

"I expect he was visiting his wife's grave. He's got a perfectly good reason to be here."

"I don't trust the whole thing," Janosch retorts. "Maybe he's just one of the staff from the school, and he'll rat on us or something."

"He won't rat on us," I tell him. "Let's go with him. Flo and the others agree—don't you?"

"We'll go with the old man," says Fat Felix. "He's okay. And no matter how you look at it, it's better than a night on a park bench. I think we'll be in good hands. You with us, Janosch?"

Janosch's face darkens. There's a harsh light in his eyes. "Can any of you tell me why *we* always land in this shit headfirst?" he wants to know.

"Because we're alive," says Florian, "and because we're young."

"That's not an argument," says Janosch.

"Of course it's an argument," says Florian. "We're here, that's all. And so long as we're here, we can always land in the shit headfirst."

"Is that how you see it, Lebert?" asks Janosch.

"That's how I see it," I say.

Fat Felix goes over to the old man. "We're coming with you. The bus should be here in five minutes."

Janosch stares up at the sky. It's quite dark already. The main street stretches away ahead of us, bleak and empty. I feel a bit uneasy. There's a sort of animal electricity. I've never done anything like this before. I think I can say the same about the end of any particular day in Neuseelen Boarding School. Everything is sort of stirred up. New. I've been here four months. Amazing how fast the time goes.

Crazy

"I know that I know nothing," Janosch suddenly lets drop. "Some philosopher once said that, didn't he?"

"Haven't a clue," I reply. "Are we supposed to know that?"

"What are we supposed to know?" asks Janosch. "That we know nothing?"

"No," I reply. "That we're supposed to know who said it."

"Oh, yes, I think we're supposed to know."

"So who said it?" I ask.

"Haven't a clue," says Janosch. "But it doesn't matter anyway. Philosophers are just bums who think they have to explain everything. But there's nothing to explain. All they have to do is take a look at the world, and they'd know that it's fucking beautiful. Their propositions are idiotic."

"You're probably right, Janosch," I say, "although *I know that I know nothing* is a pronouncement I can really use. In math, for example."

"But it isn't usually intended for that," says Janosch.

"For what then?"

"For us, of course."

"For us?"

"Yes, for us. To explain that you don't have to know anything to be crazy."

"This proposition doesn't have a thing to do with *crazy*," I reply.

"Yes it does," says Janosch. "The proposition is crazy."

"I don't understand it as a proposition," I say. "Maybe it's just too crazy. Main thing is that everything just keeps going, and we all find our own way."

"Our way to Munich?"

"Our way to wherever. Don't you want to go wherever?"

"Every place we find ourselves is *wherever*. If you just make sure they can't ever padlock your mind, then you'll always live up to *wherever*, wherever it is."

A pair of headlights shows up in the distance, coming along the main street at high speed. The square lights throw a strong wide beam onto the asphalt. The diesel engine howls as the bus pulls in at the stop. It's at least forty feet long, with rectangular advertisement panels along the sides. Some sort of mineral water touting its enticing effects. The doors open automatically. Their glass slides across the advertising panels, so that the purplish symbol of the enticing mineral water in question is now shimmering through the dark brown of the Plexiglas. We get on the bus. Florian first, then the two Felixes, Troy, and Janosch. The old man and I bring up the rear. The old man stops on the three steps leading up into the bus. Eyes bright, he turns around to me and reaches out his hand. I take it. The long rough fingernails dig into the back of my hand. I can't wait to let go of his hand again.

"I haven't even introduced myself yet," he says. "How rude of me. My name is Sambraus. Marek Sambraus. Complicated name, I know. But you don't forget it."

Sambraus turns back to the bus driver.

"Two to Rosenheim, please," he says.

The bus driver gropes for two red tickets in a drawer set next to the steering wheel and holds them out to Sambraus, who gets them stamped in a blue stamping machine. As he pushes the tickets in, it makes a pinging sound. He puts one ticket in his trouser pocket and hands the other to me. It has NEUSEELEN STOP stamped on it in blue cursive letters and the time. Seven-fifteen p.m.

Chapter 10

The others are waiting between the rows of seats. We're almost alone—there are only two other people on the bus, sitting way at the back. Lovers. They press their faces against the glass when they think no one's looking. Florian and Fat Felix keep turning around to look at them from their place just three rows in front of the couple, chosen to give them a good view. Just so that they don't miss anything. The windows are full of night. You have to struggle to make out the shapes of things. The road. Fields. The occasional hill. Typical Bavarian landscape. Troy and Skinny Felix sit together in the first row. Troy wants to be next to the window; he likes looking out into the night. Skinny Felix digs around in his backpack and pulls out a Walkman. We've got about a half hour's journey, maybe more. Depends on the traffic and the weather, but I don't think we have much to worry about tonight. Sambraus sits down by himself, right in the middle of the bus, on the aisle seat. The window obviously didn't appeal to him. But he dozes off right away anyhow. His green eyes disappear in the creases of his eyelids. His head drops onto his chest. Sambraus is asleep, breathing deeply in and out.

Janosch and I sit at the back, in the last row, right next to the pair of lovers. I get to sit at the window, which pleases me because I'll be able to think a little and calm down. Birds are flying across the dark sky. They must have a long way to go, certainly farther than we do. Though our journey is not so simple either. Janosch gets a piece of paper and pencil out of the pocket of his jeans.

I look out the window again. We're just passing some fields. The white stripes of the country road race past beneath us. On the horizon you can just see the Alps. A little section of forest interrupts the view. Huge fir trees rise up in the darkness, with a sickle moon above them that casts a faint light down onto the fields. Somewhere in the distance a thin line of smoke is rising. I think about my grandparents. They've been there for me forever, my grandfather in particular. He's one of those grandfathers you'd like to have had as your father. An unassuming old man who struggles unceasingly with life. Brave and gallant. My mother says he won't hold out much longer—at some point he'll have to give up. Cancer is really tough.

My mother loves my grandfather. Sometimes I wonder if she loves him more than she does his son, her husband. My father. But I can understand it. My grandfather is really a wonderful man. I don't want to lose him. Whenever I had problems, I'd go see him. We'd build a big fire in the fireplace—our fire. Then we would sit in front of it for three hours and talk about time. Just like that. The way everything slips by. My grandfather is a lot wiser than I am. I can't really explain a lot of what he says very coherently, but I know I'll be able to keep it in my heart until I understand it. My grandparents live in an old farmhouse outside the city. It's so beautiful. I've been there thousands of times. And I've seen my grandfather thousands of times. I won't be able to do that so often in the future. Recently there's been less wood by the fireplace.

"You got a two in German, right?" asks Janosch, looking at me pleadingly.

"No, I got a five. You know that already. I can't write essays."

"Well, anyhow, do you know how a guy tells a girl he loves her?"

"A girl? What are you doing?"

"So, I'm trying to write a love letter or something."

I laugh. "To Malen?" I ask.

"Yes, to Malen. But this stuff isn't so easy, you know. I'm not the romantic type. Every time we do dictation I make at least twenty mistakes."

"Have you ever wondered if that's why you get a six in German?"

"I haven't counted that out," answers Janosch, "but that's not interesting right now. I have to write a love letter to Malen. Everything's got so complicated. Before, all you had to do was screw a girl, then she was yours. Now you're supposed to get your fucking intellect down on paper to make an impression. But I can't get my fucking intellect down on paper. I'm not Kafka."

"Take it easy. You don't have to be Kafka. Just write what you feel."

"Should I say I feel like shit?"

"Not what you feel right now. What you feel for Malen."

"And what do I feel? That I want to fuck her?"

"No. That you love her. Just write that you love her."

"I can't," says Janosch. "She'd hit me."

"But that means she'd do the same if you were Kafka and you said *I love you.*"

"No she wouldn't. Kafka's *crazy.* And besides, girls go for literary types."

"Girls go for Leonardo DiCaprio."

"You're right about that. Should I say *I love you* as Leonardo DiCaprio?"

"You should say *I love you* as Janosch Schwarze."

"I knew that all along! You see! Writing love letters is no problem. Girls make a whole big deal out of it. Guys are different. They're crazy. No problem— their pens do automatic writing. So, what am I supposed to write?"

"Write *Malen, I love you,*" I propose.

"*Malen, I love you?* Okay."

Janosch writes on the paper with his red felt pen. His handwriting is neat and upright. You can recognize every letter.

"Now what?" he asks.

"What do you like about her most? Try to figure out what's best about her and praise it to the skies. Women like that."

"How do you do that?" asks Janosch.

"From the heart." I tell him.

"From the heart?" Janosch thinks. His eyebrows draw closer together, until they almost touch.

"I think I'd still rather fuck her," he says finally. "It's easier. Love letters are just for bums, anyhow. What my intellect can't achieve, maybe my dick can. You know that! How's your Marie, anyway?"

I lean back. "So far so good," I say. "She keeps running away from me, but aside from that, I think she's doing fine."

"Weird woman," says Janosch. "First she lets you fuck her and then she runs away from you. I don't get it."

"Yeah—I don't either. But that's how it is."

"True. All girls are alike that way. They're all strange."

"Strange and hot."

"Maybe they're hot because they're so strange?" says Janosch.

"Yes, or they're so strange because they're so hot."

Crazy

We burst out laughing, and Janosch pushes my head against the windowpane.

"Why did God make girls anyhow?" asks Janosch. "Why are they so sexy? He could just as easily have made them ugly cows and put them in the world that way."

"But that's just the point," I say. "As long as they're sexy, everyone wants to fuck them. And as long as everyone fucks them, the human race will continue. You have to admit—God's cool."

"God's *crazy*," says Janosch. "God's a sex fiend. He knew what he wanted."

"God always knows what he wants."

"And what does he want right now?" asks Janosch.

"He wants us to get to Munich in good shape," I say. "He wants us to live. And will we?"

"Of course we will," says Janosch. "We're living now. We'll always live. We'll live until there's no more living to be done."

"Are you sure?"

"Hello in there! You said so yourself. God wants us to live. And that's what we're doing. Whether we did it right or wrong is something he'll decide for himself, when we stand there in front of him."

"Will we?"

"Sometime, sure," says Janosch, "and when we do, I think I'll get his autograph."

"You want God's autograph?"

"Of course. You don't often get the chance."

"You're nuts," I say. "Do you really think God'll give you an autograph?"

"God gives everyone an autograph," says Janosch. "He's got all the time in the world and no big-star mannerisms."

"How the hell would *you* know? God is the ultimate big star. Don't you think it would be a little rude to hit him up right away for an autograph?"

"No, God would be flattered. He doesn't get that many autograph hunters."

"You're out of your mind."

Chapter 11

I look out of the window again. The dark is lifting. The harsh lights of Rosenheim penetrate the glass. We're almost there. A stray wind is gusting along the road, blowing leaves and branches into the traffic lanes. The trucks and tractor-trailers often hit their brakes. There must be a pop concert somewhere. Red laser beams are circling above the grimy town, meeting in the middle and then circling onward, crisscrossing one another. This has to be the time I find myself thinking about math. And Falkenstein, my teacher. He says he doesn't see much hope for my future. I can just forget it. No need for extra tutoring. I'm too dumb. Maybe he's right. Recently he's been asking me a lot of questions in class. Because he knows I don't understand any of it. It satisfies him somehow. It's become real psychological warfare. But that's what all of school's like. It has nothing to do with boarding school. *School* is pure psychological warfare. It's supposed to be tough. For a sixteen-year-old it's pretty hard. You're still quite young and you have the shit taken out of you accordingly by some guy who calls himself a teacher. Bavaria's particularly bad. The only ones who count here are little programmed computer kids who stuff their heads from morning to night for school. They get the encouragement. The rest are just dropped. *Knowledge is not wisdom* carries no weight here. They're all just jerk-offs like Falkenstein. On a perfectly normal day for being tested in class, he orders us to close our books. With eyes like knives he looks for a victim. By this point I've already had enough. He's threatening to call on someone to answer. At the blackboard. In front of everybody. Heaven help anyone who can't. Slowly he gets up from his chair. My forehead's sweating. I don't want to be called on to answer. Why doesn't he say right away whose turn it is? Or why doesn't he just give me a 6 right away? It would be simpler. Why does he have to torture me like this? I hate having to calculate in front of the whole class. I always make a fool of myself. I'm shaking with nerves. Falkenstein's fussy fingers tap their way across Franzen's desk. Franzi is as nervous as I am. This stuff is really difficult. And Falkenstein knows how to set the meanest exercises.

"So, Franzi?" he asks. "Are you well prepared?"

Franzi leans back and stretches his arms in front of him.

"Of course," he says very quietly. *Of course* is

good. If he'd said no, he'd have had it. If he'd said yes, it would probably have been as bad. *Of course* makes the danger pass by.

Falkenstein walks on. He toys with Melanie's pen holder. Every kid in the class wants to shove the burden of answering test questions onto someone else. Once the name of the sacrificial victim has been spoken, everyone else can feel more or less spared. A sigh of relief goes the rounds, which makes it doubly hard for the sacrificial victim. All part of the plan, I'd say. Falkenstein looks up. I tremble. Don't know one single thing anymore. The few scraps I've stored up from class are blown away by the tension. I'm ready to shit in my pants. My stomach is swelling up. My whole body has goosebumps. I'm going to be next. That's what has to be. In a deep, reverberating voice, Falkenstein says, "Lebert! Show us what I've spent all this time talking about." He always says it that way. I hate the way he says *Lebert.* As if he wants to shoot me. As if he's hauling me to the gallows. Which is what he's doing. I stand up in a sort of trance. Sweating. Empty. My mind whirls around, a blank. Only thing at its center is the piece of chalk that's been shoved into my hand. The rest of the class exhales audibly. I swallow, playing with the chalk. It feels rough. Dry. I let it move against my palm. The color comes off. My fingers are already all white. I look at the blackboard. I do not like this blackboard. You're supposed to remember everything that gets written on it. Forever. You're not allowed to forget it. And everything you write on the blackboard during a test must have been written on it at least once before. Falkenstein states a couple of theorems. I write them out. Listen to the scratchy noise the chalk makes. Now I have to work them through. Why am I standing here at all? I have no idea. I draw a figure. Two. A circle. Falkenstein's not happy. He sends me back to my seat. As I walk past the rest of the class, they look up at me and pull faces. A couple of them laugh. I glance back at my drawing on the blackboard. It looks terrible, like something out of fifth grade. I'm ashamed. Unfortunately, I can't do better. The physiotherapist, the one I see all the time, says it's because of my disability. I lack some logical function, or whatever; it's not just a physical thing. Hence my 6 in math. But it can't be that simple. I mean, everyone should be able to hack it in math, even a deadbeat like me. I'm frustrated. I pull a broken pencil out of my pencil case. It has BUILD YOUR OWN FUTURE stamped on it. Don't make me laugh! I haven't even started to build the scaffolding. So okay. I'm sixteen. Life is still ahead of me. Or that's what they say. Falkenstein arrives after class. "You can forget the school-leaving certificate," he says. "The way I see it, we should be happy if the Cultural Ministry doesn't introduce an eight just for you." He grins a great, broad grin, the corners of his mouth pulled wide almost to his ears. I'd love to smash him right in the grin. Just to see what the Cultural Ministry could really invent for me. Falkenstein leaves. I leave, too. We have a break now.

School days aren't that easy.

We're driving into Rosenheim. Traffic is heavy. Lines of cars and people everywhere. I turn to Janosch. Thoughts of our last day of tests melt away at the sight of his face. He's grinning.

"Do you think they're looking for us already?"

"I expect so," says Janosch. "They've probably just notified our parents."

"Do you think your parents are mad?"

"My parents are always mad at me," says Janosch. "But I think this isn't exactly anarchy. I already told my father one time that if I ever disappeared, I'd probably be with my friends."

"And how did he react?"

"He beat the shit out of me," says Janosch.

"He beat you? And you're still running away? I would never have believed it."

"You'd better believe it. Otherwise you won't get anywhere in life. What's that poem? 'As long as you escape both death and birth / You are a mournful ghost on a dark earth.' "

"Since when have you been interested in poetry?" I ask.

"I'm not. My brother once said it was good for picking up girls."

"You've got a brother? How old is he?"

"Twenty," says Janosch. "He lives in the States—he emigrated, or whatever. Anyhow, I like him a lot."

"Did it work?"

"Did what work?"

"The stuff with the poetry and the women?"

"Oh, that—no," says Janosch. "The girl I recited the lines to said poetry didn't do a thing for her. So unfortunately things got no farther than a milkshake."

I look out the window again. The main station, our last stop, is already visible in the distance. What will my parents say to all this? My mother must have had a panic attack. Maybe she's even driven to Neuseelen to look for me. She always gets anxious very quickly. Particularly when it's about me. She wants to protect me, never leave me on my own. I'm too vulnerable for that, in her view. If it was up to her, I'd never be in boarding school; she prefers me to be at home. With her. Where nothing terrible can happen to me. I feel so bad for her. She's probably sitting in the car right now. My father certainly has no idea about what's going on. How could he? He's living in a hotel. Recovering. Leaving is always easy, I think. But being left somehow isn't. I should be mad at him. My sister said something about there being another woman. A twenty-year-old. With big tits and long legs. If I ever meet her, I'll smack her really personally right in the mouth. I'm not too soft for that. You keep reading about that stuff in the tabloids:

Female Youth Kindles the Fires of Old Age

How Aging Husbands Regain Their Joie de Vivre

Usually there's a picture of some old granddad with a titty monster. But it can't be true. It doesn't happen in real life—just in these supermarket rags. And certainly not to me. To us. To my family. I don't want to lose them. I belong to them. What would I be without them? A piece of something? A part? Does everyone have to lose their family in order to become a person? I think I'm overthinking this. I should be making sure that I just keep going. Right now I'm somewhere in Rosenheim. The bus stops. The jolt pushes me down in my seat. I stand up. My left leg is hurting. Janosch can tell by my eyes. It's okay if I hold on to him for support, and we climb down out of the bus together. Sambraus, Florian, and the others are waiting on the sidewalk. There's a lot of activity, thousands of people walking past. They look happy. So do Florian, the two Felixes,

Troy, and Sambraus. Their faces are twitching with excitement.

"So this is it," says Fat Felix. "Off to the big city. At last the Magnificently Maddest Six of the Century are ready. Time to start for Munich."

"Do you think they've sent the police after us?" asks Janosch. His eyes are cool. He betrays no anxiety, puts an arm around me, and looks at me, almost as if he knows what I've been thinking.

"I don't believe it," says Fat Felix. "Why would they send police here of all places? They're looking for us in Neuseelen. We'll make the train with no problem at all. And then we're almost halfway home. Sambraus will get seven tickets at the ticket office out front. Nobody will pay any attention. We'll wait on the platform—I think it's number two. So we'll meet there in exactly ten minutes. Don't talk to any officials! You never know."

With these words Fat Felix and the others race off into the station, the door slamming behind them with a ringing echo. It's made of glass. The four of them go running through the entrance hall, followed by Sambraus, who walks wearily straight to the ticket booth. I look over at Janosch. He looks at my left leg.

"The usual?" he asks.

"The usual."

"You're not allowed to give up, Benni!" he

says. "A man's not allowed to give up. He can be destroyed, but he's not allowed to give up."

"Not even if it's sometimes easier to give up?" I ask.

"Not even," says Janosch firmly.

"But I want to give up," I tell him. "It's all getting too complicated. Too big. And I don't know why. I don't see the point of it, Janosch, or any end to it. I keep thinking about my parents. And my father's girlfriend. And my left leg hurts like hell. A lame leg doesn't go very well with the maddest journey of the century. A lame leg goes well with sleeping a lot and resting. I'm tired, Janosch, really tired."

"Benjamin Lebert—you're a hero," says Janosch in a deep voice. There's a glint in his eyes. He slowly pulls me a step farther.

"A hero? Cripples are heroes?"

"Not cripples—*you*."

"Why?"

"Because life speaks through you."

"Through me?"

"Through you."

"What speaks through me is all crap."

"No—it's exciting!" Janosch says exultantly, full of delight. "Life's exciting—there's always something new."

"Is that what we want?"

"Of course it's what we want," Janosch shouts. "Otherwise it would be boring. We must always be searching for—what did Felix call it?—the thread. That's it, the thread. You have to keep searching for the thread. Youth is nothing but one long thread hunt. Come on, Benni! Let's find it! With luck it'll be on the train to Munich."

And with that he pushes me into the train station.

Chapter 12

Inside there's a big hall, with ticket booths and information desks in the middle. Big blue letters hang above them, spelling out directions. A despairing voice echoes from the loudspeaker, "Number twenty-seven-D, please come to booth A." Janosch looks up and laughs. I wonder who poor number 27-D is. The walls are covered in advertising posters. Mostly ads for daily newspapers. I look for my uncle's and find it all the way over to the right, close to the ceiling. The type glows down at us. You can see the tracks in the distance. Our train leaves from platform 2. It's already posted:

IC 134 to Karlsruhe. Intermediate stops at Munich, Pasing, Stuttgart. Estimated time of departure: 8:45 P.M.

I look up at the clock. It's 8:32. There's still time. Janosch runs to one of the tobacconists that line the hall. More of a tobacco kiosk, really. A short, pale man peers out through an open window, above which hangs a neon sign, shaped like a cigarette, that says MONSIEUR DE TABAC.

"What d'you want?" I ask Janosch as he heads for the little window.

"Two cigars."

"Two cigars? What for?"

"For us," says Janosch. "To smoke."

"Us? Why?"

"Because we're men. And men smoke cigars," he replies. "Didn't you ever see *Independence Day*?"

"Sure. But those guys saved the world from extra-terrestrials. We're not there yet."

"No, we're not there yet," says Janosch, "but we've done something sort of the same."

"Just what, may I ask?"

"We broke out of school, which was just as hard for us as saving the world from extraterrestrials. You have to see things in their proper perspective."

"You really think so?"

"Sure," says Janosch. "Besides, we've earned a cigar. *Basta*."

So saying, he steps up to the short pale man in the window.

"Guys! Can anyone tell me why I let myself be schlepped along?" asks Fat Felix as we're standing on the platform. It's 8:42. The train will be here any minute.

"Maybe because we're friends," is Janosch's explanation.

"Friends?" croaks Fat Felix. "So what's friendship?"

Janosch thinks. "Friendship is something inside you," he says finally. "You can't see it, but it's there all the same."

"Yes, it's there all the same," interjects Skinny Felix. "Just the way a day is."

"A day?" asks Fat Felix. "If friendship is supposed to be like a day, what the hell does that make the sun?"

"Us, of course," says Skinny Felix. "We're the sun."

"We're the sun?" asks Janosch. "So what revolves around us?"

"Friendship," says Skinny Felix. "At least that's my view."

"And who casts the light?" asks Janosch. "Am I the one who casts the light?"

"We all cast the light," says Skinny Felix. "We all cast our light into our friendship."

"I don't get it," says Florian a.k.a. Girl. "So does anyone see our light?"

"We see it," says Glob, "and that's enough."

"Nobody else?" asks Florian.

"Depends on how big the friendship is," says Skinny Felix. "Sometimes other people see it too. But we're the ones who have to see it first. Because a thing has to be lit up before you can see it. That's what this is about: friendship is something like lighting things up."

"All this stuff about lighting things and not lighting things is a crock of shit," says Janosch. "Our friendship is crazy, that's all. And besides, it's what brought us here."

"Just friendship?" asks Florian.

"Well, maybe Glob's roast pork too," says Janosch. "But apart from that it was our friendship—I mean, it has to have been something. Does anyone feel like swearing blood brotherhood? I've got some sort of thumbtack in my pants pocket. That would do."

"I don't know," says Fat Felix. "We're not doing Robin Hood here. Besides, we've done enough insane things for one evening already. Let's lay off."

"You can never do enough insane things," says Janosch. "You have to drink life."

"Drink it?" asks Florian a.k.a. Girl. "Does that mean life's a river?"

"Something like that," says Skinny Felix.

"Are you guys out of your skulls?" asks Janosch. "We're the sun? Life's a river? Friendship revolves around us? Enough already! Life is life. A river is a river. And if I didn't know better, I'd say friendship is just friendship. Why do we keep trying to explain all that in pictures? Why do we always have to understand everything? Does God even want us to understand things? I think God really just wants us to get on and live."

"Have you suddenly got religion?" Fat Felix turns to Janosch.

"Sort of, yes," says Janosch. "It's Lebert's fault. All that yammering on about life. And yes, I'd absolutely believe in God before I believed that life is a river. Life is an attempt."

"And what are we attempting?" asks Florian.

"We're attempting to attempt everything," says Janosch. "That's the attempt. So now let's attempt to become blood brothers. Girl, you're first!"

Florian steps forward, looking doubtful. He sticks out a finger.

"Do any of you have AIDS?" he asks.

"Me, of course," says Fat Felix. "Didn't you know?"

"Cut the crap," says Florian. "This thumbtack's going to hurt."

"It's not going to hurt at all," says Janosch. "And besides, you're a man." And he sticks the thumbtack into his own forefinger. The blood bubbles up. Then he does the same to Florian, who winces. They rub their forefingers together. Janosch makes the rounds. He sticks the pin in Troy, then in Glob and Felix. Then in me. A little stab goes through my body. I can't stand the sight of blood. It makes me queasy. I turn away as Janosch presses our fingers together. Once we're all done, we put our hands on one another's. Blood brothers.

The train is five minutes late. The first sign of it is a piercing whistle that comes rolling at us out of the distance. Then the train pulls into the Rosenheim station. It's an ordinary red intercity express. I don't see many people through the windows. Most of them are standing by the doors, ready to get out. The train hisses to a stop. The doors slide open slowly. Lots of tourists get out onto the platform.

Sambraus pulls the tickets from his raincoat and gives them to us. We're in luck. Our train car is number 29 and we're standing at car number 22. Glob, Troy, Florian, and Felix go first, with Janosch, Sambraus, and me behind. Janosch is holding me up. I'm worn out, somehow. We've barely reached number 29 when a black-uniformed conductor pulls us onto the train. He's a little man with a terrific mop of white hair. The door closes and the train slowly starts to move.

"Friends, huh?" says the conductor as he notices Janosch holding me up.

"Yes, friends," says Janosch and pushes me into the compartment where the other five are sitting. Troy has already made himself comfortable, still wearing the rain cape. His eyes are closed and he's breathing heavily. Maybe he's dreaming of a better world. Opposite him is Sambraus, who's pulled a book out of his pocket: Paul Auster's *Leviathan*. A paperback with the head of the Statue of Liberty on the front. As far as I can tell, Sambraus is about halfway through. I don't know the book. I don't know the author either. Only his name is familiar to me. Paul Auster. One of the handful of great authors or something. But there are thousands of those already. Next to Sambraus is Florian, staring out the window. His face looks tired; his mind must be far away. Maybe with his dead parents. Or his grandmother. Now he's looking at the floor. He stretches his arms out in front of him uneasily. On his right is Skinny Felix. His chest is heaving, and his nostrils are pinched. He keeps running his left hand over his right forefinger. He's trying to rub the blood away. His finger's all sticky and doesn't look so good, sort of like he was having a nosebleed or something. Glob is right at the end. He's parked his big ass squarely on the seat and is busy with his backpack of goodies. Gummi Bears come into view. Yellow, red, purple. In all their multicolored glory they follow one another into Glob's hamster cheeks, where they get worked into porridge. Now and then his greedy tongue pops out of his mouth. It's bright pink from the candy. Janosch and I sit down on the right of the car next to Troy. I get to take the window seat again, which I like. Black night outside. Only the moon shines down on us from up there. Occasionally a few fir trees loom up in the darkness. Otherwise a great barren plain. You can see almost nothing.

The tracks that race parallel to ours curve away to the left, ending our shared journey to Munich. I slide down deeper and deeper in my seat. It's comfortable; you could go to sleep in it. There's a picture hanging above every seat. Most are of some scene in the history of railroads. Mine is an advertisement for an English-language course. TALK THE WORDS RIGHT OUT OF YOUR SOUL or some such. I look over at Janosch. His eyes are hidden. Something's going on in him. His hands jerk unpredictably on the armrests. They're delicate: you can see almost every vein forking. A few blond hairs glint on their backs. The dim light in the compartment shows up every one. Janosch's fingers move over his black polo shirt. A look of freedom flickers on his face. He's looking forward to Munich. I look out of the window again. Out on the dark horizon someone's flying a plane, red lights blinking. Where is he taking his passengers? Closer, by the tracks, four kids have made a fire and are sitting comfortably on a rise, smoking. We race past them. I find myself thinking about my last school and the people I got to know there, who always called me Crookfoot because I walked so funny, with my left foot always dragging behind. They didn't like that. Sometimes they'd stick out a leg and laugh when I fell on my face. And sometimes they waited for me outside school, to take the sandwich I'd brought for my break. Made by my mother, especially for me, with lots of cheese and sausage. It made me feel bad for her. I didn't want to hand over the sandwich, ever. But I had to; they were stronger than I am. Matthias Bochow was the ringleader. A heavy-set guy with huge shoulders and brown curly hair, no more than five foot eight. He'd been on earth for seventeen years already, and there wasn't a thing on it that he smelled, saw, or felt that he liked. And whatever he didn't like, the rest of them didn't like either. He was the leader, the bellwether. His will was law, and the law was hard. The other five kids were only hangers-on. Peter Trimolt was seventeen; Michael Wiesbeck, eighteen; Stephan Genessius, seventeen; Claudio Bertram, seventeen; and Karim Derwert, sixteen. They did Matthias's dirty work. Whatever he wanted was carried out. They got him women, got him through eleventh grade, and got the dipshits out of his way. Dipshits like me—Crookfoot. One time they tied me to a tree after school, a beech. With some old vine cording they'd stolen from the caretaker. Left me to survive until early evening, when my mother came running into the school yard in tears, beside herself. She didn't let me go back to school for two weeks. It was great—at least I could get myself together again. Read a little. I think Matthias Bochow's still around somewhere. I sometimes see him down in the subway with some hot chick. But he doesn't notice me.

I reach for my backpack and get a bar of chocolate and my book. There are a couple of stars visible outside. The airplane has disappeared. I hold the book in both hands and run my thumbs over it. The cover feels smooth and good to the touch. I love just running my hand over books—it gives you such a calming feeling, a feeling that there really is something in the world you can hold on to, even though everything's racing by so fast. I get this feeling particularly with new books. And this is a new book. My father gave it to me. It's a paperback. He says it's the best book anyone's ever written about life. The receipt is still sticking out of the back—7.90 deutsche marks. *Thank you for your purchase. Lehmkuhl, your bookseller.* My father got it for me the last time I was home for the weekend. It still smells quite new. Nice smell. It has a red cover, and on it there's an old man with his arm around a little kid, and there's a big bar jutting into the picture from one side that says *Nobel Prize.* The book must have got an award—no idea if it's a big one or not, but so what. Over on the right, in cramped white letters, it says *The Old Man and the Sea, by Ernest Hemingway.* Great title. You know immediately there's something going on, and you want to start reading right away. Which is what I do.

Crazy

I open the book slowly, holding it in my right hand, because my left hand's no use anyway; it's thin and looks awful and slips into its usual spasm. I begin to read. Take a quick check on the time: 9:19. We've got about seventy minutes to go. Time enough. I keep reading. The letters and sentences fly at me. It's a wonderful book. Every phrase, every observation strike home. It's not long before there are tears in my eyes. Which is the way it is with me. Give me a good book and I start to howl. I howled my way through *Treasure Island* and now I'm howling my way through *The Old Man and the Sea*. It's the way I'm made. The story's pretty simple; it's only fifty pages. It's about this old fisherman who's on his last legs and just can't seem to catch any more fish. He goes hungry. Everyone's laughing at him. The only one on his side is a small boy who always used to go out fishing with him, but now he's not supposed to anymore because his parents won't let him. The old man doesn't catch enough, so the old man has to go out alone. And one day he gets this huge fish on his line. But he struggles to land it until he's exhausted, and he loses the catch of his life to the sea and the sharks. It's a really fabulous book. I'm only a quarter of the way into it and I'm in tears already. I'm so moved I'm clutching the book to my chest. I thank my father for buying it for me. And I thank Ernest Hemingway for being able to tell a story like that. I blow my nose in a handkerchief.

Janosch looks over at me and he's laughing.

"That's the way Lebert is, when you get right down to it," he explains, turning to Sambraus. "A bit on the sensitive side.

"So what were you reading?" Janosch asks.

"The Old Man and the Sea."

"The Old Man and the Sea?" Janosch folds his hands. "It's supposed to be pretty good. Maybe you can read a bit of it to me—for fun. We've still got a ways to go, and besides, I'd like to have encountered real literature."

"Is it literature?"

"I think so."

"So what's literature?"

"Literature is where you read a book and feel you could put a little mark under every line because it's true."

"Because it's true? I don't get it."

"When every sentence is simply right. When it reveals something about the world. And life. When every phrase gives you the feeling that you would have behaved or thought exactly the same way the character in the book does. That's when it's literature."

"Where did you get that from?"

"I just think so, that's all."

"You just think so? Then for sure it's shit. I bet a literature professor would say something else. How many books have you read already anyhow?"

"Maybe two."

"Maybe two? And you're telling me about literature?"

"Well, you wanted to hear it, and besides, the whole thing's too complicated. Not even the people who're supposed to understand it understand anything. So why should *we* beat our brains out? Let's just read for the fun of it, and for the fun of getting it, and stop wondering if it's literature or not. Other people can take care of that. If it really is literature, all the better. And if it isn't, who the fuck cares?"

"My view completely," I say and open the paperback again. A high-pitched whistle comes out of the loudspeakers, then the voice of the conductor. It's all distorted and gets cut off quite often, but we get the gist of it. We'll be half an hour late into Munich. Janosch and the others sigh. I give myself over to my text and read it loudly and clearly, only making occasional mistakes. Other times I don't read so well, and I always hesitate in class. I hate it when we have to read aloud. But here it goes okay. Soon Janosch isn't the only one listening; the others have pricked up their ears as well and they're gaping at me wide-eyed. Even Sambraus seems to be enjoying it. The Paul Auster book slips down between the armrests, and he folds his hands on his stomach. I don't know how long I read, but it's a damn long time. My mouth is dry and empty. The old man loses the battle with the sea. Comes back home empty handed. The guys' faces are all red. Even Janosch is sniffling out loud. He shakes his head furiously and his eyes are almost bursting and his ears have turned dark red on the inside. He makes a hasty grab for the novel.

Glob and Skinny Felix are so upset they reach for each other's hands, and there are tears in their eyes. Troy and Florian stay cool. I guess they don't think much of it, and they're showing no emotion. Now Fat Felix reaches for the book and leafs quickly through it to read the most important bits again. Then he gives it back to me. His face is alight. I check the time: ten-forty. We should be in Munich soon.

Chapter 13

Fat Felix raises his voice as he looks out the window. "Do you think we're as brave as the old man in the book?" he asks. "Even when everything is about loss?"

"We're all brave," says Janosch.

"But why are we?" is Fat Felix's question. "Where's the dividing line between *valiant* and *brave*?"

"There is no dividing line," says Florian a.k.a. Girl. "Everyone's both valiant and brave."

"How?" says Fat Felix.

"Because everyone wakes up in the morning and sets off into life," is Skinny Felix's contribution, "without blowing their brains out. Which is valiant *and* brave."

"So why doesn't anyone see it or say so?" asks Glob.

"Because it's become self-evident," says Janosch.

"Self-evident?" Fat Felix wants to know. "Why is everything in the world self-evident? Why is everything always assumed in advance? That we set off into life. That we put one foot in front of the other.

Why is it so normal? Which damn book says so? And who was the asshole who published it?"

"The asshole's name is God," says Sambraus, frowning.

Fat Felix thinks Sambraus is an okay guy; he had a great conversation with him in Rosenheim, all about life and his future.

Sambraus was at school in Neuseelen. He had an absolutely terrible time there, felt locked in, just wanted to go back home. And then when he did get home, nothing worked anymore. He suddenly missed the orderly life of boarding school. In the Second World War he was on the Russian front. After the war ended, he and his fiancée, whom he'd met on leave, moved to Neuseelen. And that's where they got married. Then in 1977 his wife died. Cancer. He buried her in the cemetery at Neuseelen, because she loved the place so much. After that, Sambraus obviously flipped out. Went to brothels and so on. Just screwed away his misery. He even moved to an apartment in Munich right above a strip joint. Still lives there. And for the last twenty years he's been going out to her grave in Neuseelen every second day with a big bunch of red roses, her favorite flower.

"Why does God do things like that?" asks Glob, clenching his fists.

"Because everything in the world has to unwind according to a certain scheme of things," is Sambraus's explanation. "And the scheme is you have to see in order to see, hear in order to hear, understand in order to understand. And move on, in order to move on. So move, boy, move!"

Fat Felix presses his face against the windowpane, making big, dark patches form on the glass. Out of the loudspeakers comes the scratchy voice of the conductor. *In a few minutes we shall be arriving at the main station in Munich.*

Outside the windows is Munich. I stand at the door with Janosch, Troy, and the others behind me as we roll into the main station. Glob's big backpack almost gets stuck on the way out of the compartment. Next to us there's a blond man with a tired-looking German shepherd.

"Now's the time," says Janosch.

"Time for what?" I ask.

"The cigars," says Janosch. "We're coming into Munich, and now's the time to smoke them. Big heroes, like in *Independence Day*."

He pulls them out of his pocket. They're cheap cigars—Agnos. But who cares? He hands me one and sticks the other in his mouth, waits till I do the same, then lights them. He's indifferent to the NO SMOKING sign. The blond man doesn't interest him either. He draws greedily on his cigar. The blond man winks. I turn away and blow smoke into a little recessed area. The cigar tastes foul, and I'll be glad when I've finished it. The German shepherd sneezes. I feel sorry for him. His gentle eyes are watching me. I turn around again.

"Are you afraid of death?" I ask Janosch.

"No one who's young is afraid of death," he says.

"Really?"

"Really. Anyone who's young only begins to be afraid of death when he's not young anymore. Until then, all he has to do is live. So he doesn't think about death."

"So why am *I* afraid of death?" I ask.

"It's something else," says Janosch.

"So what is it?"

"With you it's the sea," says Janosch.

"The sea?"

"The sea of anxiety. You've got to get rid of it. You know, your world is full of things that are out to kill you. Your parents' divorce. School. Other guys. Try to be sure you don't kill yourself! It would be a pity!"

Janosch pulls on his cigar. I look up at him. I admire him. I've never said it to him, but I admire him. Janosch is life. He's light; he's the sun. If there is a God, he talks through Janosch. I know it. And he should give him his blessing.

The train comes to a halt. We're here. The doors open, and the first one out onto the platform is the blond man with the dog. Then it's me and Janosch. I see the dog disappearing into the crowd. He's sweet. He's got his muzzle pointed toward the ground, and he stumbles wearily and discontentedly beside his companion. The last I see of him is his tail, a bushy scrap of hair, also pointing toward the ground.

It makes me think of our dog, Charlie. He was part Saint Bernard. His father was a monster and so was his mother, so it's no wonder he grew to stand about three foot six. He died two years ago. It seems an eternity. Charlie was my friend and a big support when things got tough. Sometimes I would lie with him at night when I couldn't get to sleep and there was a storm outside. I hated storms. They left Charlie totally cold. He was a rock, and I could hide behind him whenever and wherever I needed to. I'll never forget the way he snuffled. His nose would squeeze itself together like a sponge. It felt soft. Everything about him felt soft. His ears were like cotton wool, and his stomach was a big ship rising and falling according to the weather. I remember our last night together. Charlie had thrown up blood again. I slept with him in the bathroom on a deck chair. But I couldn't stand that for very long. I crawled down next to him and went back to sleep on a towel. Charlie had a pretty shitty night. His breath rattled and he vomited blood. All I could do for him was to be there and put an arm around him, which I did—I put my arm around him and prayed. I prayed I wouldn't lose my dog. Charlie had always protected me. Nobody called me a cripple when he was around. I could rely on that. I used to take him on extra-long walks through areas where lots of other kids lived. And the ones who saw me treated me with respect because I had him, Charlie. My dog and my rock. Whenever I was lonely, we played a game with a ring, a plastic one about four inches wide, which I threw in the air for Charlie to catch. The whole thing was pretty boring, but that was the game, our game. Sometimes we played all day. That night two years ago when our dog died, God wasn't on the case, and he didn't hear me. Charlie died around four in the morning. The great big ship rose and fell one last time, then stopped in mid-movement. His eyes went dim. He was the same age as I was. Fourteen. When we got him, I was a baby. But I still remember him. And as long as I do, Charlie will stay alive, in some way or other. We buried him in a field that same day. The whole family was there and everyone cried except for my mother, who didn't particularly like Charlie. She always saw him as a big danger to me, and besides, he was a lot of work. My father on the other hand really liked him, and they had a great relationship. It was my father who named him after Charlie Watts, the drummer for the Rolling Stones. If our dog was still alive, I'd go visit him, but that's all over now. Time pays no heed to me or Charlie. My rock.

"Isn't that the taste of life?" asks Janosch, pulling on his Agno cigar. The others are now out on the platform. I can see from their eyes that they're a little exhausted. Wearily they join the surge of people. The platform's bigger than the one at Rosenheim, at least thirty-three feet wide, and it stretches a good hundred yards or more. The surface is stone, which makes every step give off a strange clacking sound. Fat Felix likes it and laughs as he stamps his right foot on the ground. There are still a lot of people around at this hour. Mostly kids, dawdling along the platform in pairs or groups. Some of them to smoke or drink, some of them just to be here, meet other kids, piss on the daily grind. A couple of homeless guys are lying on the ground in front of an advertising panel. Their lives show in their faces. Covered in scratches and scars. One of them looks up at me. He has long white hair and a reddish beard. He drops an arm over his companion. They'll both be asleep in a minute. I give them a little money—I can't just go by without leaving anything. I turn back to Janosch and the others. They are repaying Sambraus the ticket money he laid out for them.

"I always thought life tasted different," I say, taking a drag on my Agno cigar. The smoke is deep and dark as it rises.

"So, how did you think it tastes?" asks Janosch.

"Maybe a little sweet. There are a few sweet things in life too."

"Where did you come up with this shit? At best, sweet is what my chocolate snail tastes like, not life," Glob interrupts. "Have you guys noticed how much shit we've been talking lately?"

"We always talk shit," says Skinny Felix.

"Yes," says Glob, "but we're not here to talk shit, we're here to *do* shit—so let's go!"

"Glob's right," says Janosch. "Come on, let's go."

So we take off through the entrance hall of the main station. It's pretty big. Shops everywhere. Even a porno movie theater. Fat Felix presses his nose up to a movie poster. *House of Lusts*. There's a black woman on the poster with her legs spread. All she's got on is a pair of red panties. A white band covers her chest. Glob thinks it's shameless and starts grousing.

"Come on," says Janosch. "We're on our way to a strip joint after all! It'll have real women. If you've got the hots, just hang on."

"My hots can take care of themselves," retorts Fat Felix, and stays looking at the poster. We start moving again, with Sambraus in front. Then Skinny Felix and Janosch. Florian, Troy, and I are at the back.

Troy pulls a face and his eyes are sparkling.

"So, do you like it?" I ask.

"Yes, I like it. I'd like to stay here forever."

"In Munich?"

"No—with you guys. I'm slowly beginning to feel I'm alive."

"Nicely put."

Florian a.k.a. Girl runs quickly to catch up with the others.

"Troy can talk," I hear him yelling excitedly in the hall.

"Really?"

The others turn around. Fat Felix comes out of the back part of the hall.

Chapter 14

"Do you have a disability pass?" Janosch asks me as we get into the subway. We only have four stations to go, to München Freiheit. It doesn't take long. There's practically nobody else in the car. We sit down.

"No," I say.

"Why not?" Fat Felix wants to know.

"They won't give me one. They say I'm not disabled. I can walk, that's their opinion."

"Are they out of their minds?" asks Janosch. "Don't they examine you?"

"No, but I have to admit I'm not all that keen on this disability pass. What do I need it for? Just to prove I'm a cripple?"

"You just told me yourself the other day that you have problems with your balance," says Janosch. "That kind of thing can be dangerous—in the subway, for example, when it's full of people. That's why there are these seats reserved for the disabled. They're made especially for you!"

"And besides, you could get in almost everywhere

cheaper," adds Fat Felix. "Take the porno theaters, to begin with!"

"You've earned it, that's all," says Janosch. "You've got a bum deal with your disability, you know? They could easily give you compensation. But of course what do they care? Typical government."

"It's not the government, it's the social services," I point out.

"So what, it's the same kind of guys. Government."

"What do you mean by government?" asks Fat Felix.

"Nobody can really define it," is Florian's view. "Something like the people who take care of everything, I think. Who decide what's just and unjust."

"And what's the point of them?" asks Fat Felix.

"Well, they do build roads and stuff," says Janosch. "And subways. Without them we wouldn't be sitting here."

"But aren't they the same people responsible for all the conspiracies?" asks Glob. "The people who refuse to tell us that there are *aliens*?"

"Yes, they're the same ones, I think," says Florian. "And they're also the ones who put people in jail."

"Shit, what else are they up to?" asks Fat Felix. "This stuff is really bad. What part do we get to play in this whole plot?"

"We're the people," says Skinny Felix.

"So what are the others, if we're the people?" asks Glob.

Skinny Felix thinks. His eyes roll; he meshes his hands together. "The others are the *big* people," he says finally.

"The *big* people?" Glob repeats. "Like in conspiracy movies?"

"Come on," says Janosch. "A film's a film. Reality is something else again."

"But movies are crazy," says Fat Felix. "Did any of you see *Pulp Fiction*?"

"Everybody's seen *Pulp Fiction*," says Janosch. "And it wasn't that fantastic."

"So what's a better one?" asks Florian.

"*Braveheart*," says Janosch. "It's good. Mel Gibson's *crazy*. And besides, I like Scotland."

"Why Scotland in particular?" I ask.

"Well—lots of plants."

"Lots of plants? So you think heaven has lots of plants?"

"Heaven has everything," says Janosch, "and so does Scotland. The weather protects the country from the people."

"How?" says Fat Felix.

"Because it never stops raining," Janosch explains.

"And since when did you start wanting to get away from people?" asks Skinny Felix.

"Since it got too crowded here," says Janosch. "Everything here's just too cramped. I sometimes feel like I can't breathe anymore. Horrible feeling. I don't have it in Scotland. In Scotland I'm free."

Crazy

"Maybe we should go to the movies together sometime," says Fat Felix.

"Why are you suddenly so keen on the movies?" asks Janosch.

"Well, movies tell you about life, don't they?"

"I think the road to the movies tells you more," says Janosch.

"Do you guys know what I've realized after this conversation?" I ask.

"Lebert has had a realization," says Janosch.

"So what is it?" asks Fat Felix.

"The world is *crazy*."

"You're right about that," says Janosch. "Crazy and wonderful. And we should use every second we've got in it."

The others slap me on the back.

Chapter 15

The strip joint with Sambraus's apartment right above it would have to be called Lebert's Iron Bar. The guys are laughing as I come through the door with Sambraus. I've talked a bit to him on the way here. About life. And his life. He would like to track down his old friend from boarding-school days. Xavier Mils. He'll look for him later in the phone book. Apparently we are very like him, Janosch in particular. Sambraus said Mils would certainly enjoy meeting us. But they haven't come across each other in years. So it's time they did.

Sambraus strikes me as a nice guy. Even Janosch has come around to this view. The two of them talked a little on the subway. On the other hand, Glob still thinks Sambraus is a maniac—but a nice maniac. He's probably right. And he's probably done quite a lot of things in his life. You can see right away, just from where he lives. The strip joint is on a side street, an old three-story building. The walls are gray and peeling. Above the second floor is a neon sign with the aforesaid inscription, LEBERT'S IRON BAR. The script is three-dimensional, with the pink letters jammed in tight together. Next to it you can see the shape of a naked woman, also made of neon, that moves its arms and legs. They shine in the car headlights.

"Why didn't you tell us that you'd gone into the porn business," asks Janosch, shouting with laughter.

"It was meant to be a surprise," I tell him.

"You succeeded!" says Fat Felix.

"Lebert's Iron Bar. Benjamin, you're crazy."

And with that we go into the strip joint. The air inside is thick. I can hardly breathe, and gasp in desperation. There's a white mist floating over the floor. The walls are pink. Every four feet a picture of a naked woman in a neon frame. Green. To the right there's a stage, maybe seven feet high. Black. To both the left and the right is an iron pole that runs from the ceiling to the floor of the stage. A red curtain marks the back of the stage, and hanging down over it is a small advertising panel showing seconds ticking by. From 60 to 0. Right now it's at 53. Opposite the stage is the bar. A big, broad-shouldered man is standing behind it dispensing drinks. He has a full brown beard and quick little eyes. His eyebrows are thick and bushy, and there are lots of creases on his forehead. Behind the huge man are rows and rows of bottles. Mostly whiskey, wine, and other alcoholic stuff. There are five men sitting at the bar, looking weary and defeated, staring at the signboard, which has now reached 49. There must be about fifty people in here. It's pretty crowded. They're all sitting on bar stools at high round tables in the middle of the room. Most of them have their legs crossed. They keep sneaking glances at the sign-board: 45. The loudspeakers are droning music from the seventies. A DJ who seems to be around twenty is playing the records. His hair is of course bleach blond. He's wearing a black leather suit with a white SIMPLY RED T-shirt peeking out now and then. His face is smooth and unlined. In front of him are two turntables, with piles of records and a microphone beside them. He has black earphones on. "It's All Right" by Supertramp is coming out of the loud-speakers. The signboard is now showing 42. The broad-shouldered man at the bar looks up as he sees us coming. His glance moves to Sambraus. Then he smiles.

"Sammy! Who've you dragged in with you?" he asks.

"Six boys from Neuseelen Boarding School," says Sambraus. "They took off today. So I thought I'd bring them to dear Martin so that they finally get something to see for once. These here are Janosch, Troy, Felix, Florian, another Felix, and Benni! Boys—meet the honorable Martin Lebert!"

"Martin Lebert?" says Janosch. "It's my pleasure," and roars with laughter.

The signboard is showing 31.

"Boys, you're welcome," says Lebert. "Tonight we'll make it a real party. If you have any requests, just tell me. What do you want to drink?"

"Bacardi O all around," says Janosch.

"On my bill," adds Sambraus.

"Thanks," says Glob, "but I do have a question."

"Ask away," says Martin Lebert in his deep voice.

"Would it be possible, do you think, to get some roast pork?"

"Roast pork?" Lebert repeats. "You're in a strip joint."

"I know," says Glob, "but you might just have some anyway. I'm—kind of hungry."

"Okay, let me see what can be done. But first, here are your Bacardis."

He sets them out on the bar. Tall red glasses with straws and bits of lemon swimming around. The guys slam down the drinks as fast as they can. Sambraus pays. I take my time.

A half-naked lady comes over to us. She's wearing blue-and-white panties with stripes of red sequins. Her top just covers her nipples and is made of blue fur. There are pieces of red confetti twinkling in her long brown hair. Her face is delicate and strikingly made-up.

"Sammy! Who are these cute guys with you?" she asks.

The signboard shows 22.

"Oh, Laura," says Sambraus, "great to see you again. They're from boarding school and they're on the run. I brought them here with me."

"They're really nice-looking guys," says Laura. "Particularly that one!" and she points at me, and comes over waggling her big tits, and strokes my hair.

"In a couple of years you'll be a great-looking guy, you know that?"

Her voice is soft. I look down her cleavage. The rest of the guys are enthralled and staring. Must be the Bacardi giving them courage. Janosch puts an arm around Laura's waist.

"Will you be up onstage at some point, too?" he asks expectantly.

"Yes, I will. Right after Angélique. I'll be dancing just for you, sweet guys!"

Janosch's ears turn dark red, and he stares at the floor.

"Laura, don't spoil my boys," says Lebert, and laughs.

"I won't. I have to go anyhow. So—be well, and have a great time, sweet guys. And don't get too close to Sammy here: he's a tiger!"

She laughs and disappears into the crowd. Her panties are almost nonexistent in the back. You can see her behind. I would like to sink into it. The rest of the guys feel the same. We all stare after her. Sam-

braus and Lebert are laughing. Her behind is a little
tanned, and it's high. The cheeks of her ass almost
stick together. It looks sexy. The signboard is showing a big 10, bigger than the other numbers. Janosch
sticks his arms up in the air.

"Finally," he yells. "Thank you, God, that I'm
alive!" and orders another round of Bacardis. Lebert
doesn't ask how old we are; all he does is smile. He's
probably just having a good day. He pours the Bacardi. I have to drain my glass as quick as I can. It
makes me feel weird. Everything's going around. I
gasp. The others have already finished their second
round. I actually mean to just raise my glass, but Fat
Felix tips it down my throat. Everything inside me
goes warm. I can feel my heart beating. It's like a
sledgehammer. I sneeze. Think about Laura. And
my mother. I hope she's okay. And I hope she's not
worrying too much. I could go see her now. But I
don't; there wouldn't be any point. Suddenly everything goes dark. The signboard shows a big 1. I sway
forward and then back. Janosch yells out again. At
least four arms come around me, and the weight of
at least six people pushes me toward the stage. Fat
Felix pours something else down my throat. Tastes
like beer, but with an aftertaste. The DJ's clear voice
comes out of the loudspeakers and hammers its way
into my head. *"And now for the fifth time for you
tonight: Angélique!"* Michael Jackson's "The Way

You Make Me Feel" is boiling under my feet. The guys are screaming. I'm headed up into the air. I stumble. I see Janosch's face.

"Lebert, I won't forget this evening, I can tell you! And I won't forget your name either!"

He runs his hand through my hair and smiles. I've never seen Janosch smile like that before, and I'll never see him smile like that again. Troy has joy nailed all over his face with big fat pushpins. Even Fat Felix is laughing. He leaps into the air, hauling me with him. He can't wait for Angélique. She's wearing a man's black suit. Her hips are swiveling. Her hair is black and reaches to her neck. Her face is soft and clear, with small twinkling brown eyes. She's hardly more than five feet tall. She's wearing high heels. Black suede. She insinuates her leg around one of the iron poles. Undoes her pants. Slides down the pole. Hoarse yelling from the audience. Janosch is yelling too. He runs his hands through his hair, grabs Felix's back. We're jumping in the air. Angélique is wearing black panties under her trousers. She licks her finger and lets it wander inside. Plays a little. Her brown eyes roll. I get a hard-on. It's pressing against my jeans.

I feel fantastic. Everything's going around in circles. I don't give a shit about anything. My father's big-breasted friend. My mother's anxieties. My sister's love. All I want is to get onto the stage and get to

Angélique. And lick her ass. Janosch shoves a ten-mark note into my hand.

"Bet you won't have the guts to go up onstage and stick this in her panties."

"And if I do?" I ask.

"Together?"

"Together."

We push through the rows. I'm already seeing everything in triplicate. Janosch holds me up. We're shaking. We come to a halt in front of the stage.

Angélique has thrown away her jacket. All she's wearing is a small bikini top. Her skin is glistening. I almost come. I can no longer feel the ground under my feet. Janosch grabs my shoulder and tries to make eye contact with Angélique. My head's on fire. The bikini top lands on the floor. I see Angélique's tits. I'm ready to die. They're like two peaches, round and beautiful, with dark red nipples. The audience is roaring. Florian and the others come rushing to the front. Fat Felix tips another something down my throat. It tastes of anise and burns in my gullet. Florian and Troy push me up onto the stage. Janosch comes flying into the middle of it from behind. The audience is laughing. The ten-mark note is shaking in my hand. Now I'm down on my knees. Angélique's navel is undulating in front of me. I see the sweat on her skin, can almost smell it. Angélique puts my hands on her hips. They sink right in. Her tits seem to spread out left and right.

My forehead bumps against her stomach. Somewhere in the back of the audience a furious old man is on his feet.

"Whose children are those? Get them off the stage!"

Sambraus raises a hand. "They belong to me."

The furious man goes silent and sullenly sits back down on his bar stool.

"So do it!" says Janosch. His voice is trembling and he's shaking his head like mad, looking back over his shoulder. His hand runs over the floor. "We can do it."

Slowly he gets to his feet. I rub my hand around Angélique's navel and the ten-mark note follows its every move. Slowly I inch lower. Stick my little finger in her panties. Pull them away a little from her skin. Janosch takes a deep breath. I pull the panties way down and throw in the money. For a moment I leave my finger where it is. I look at Angélique's cunt, which I can see only in a blur. Her pubic hair is black. Shaved to a point. Janosch bends over me and takes a look inside the panties too. I remove my little finger and let go of the panties, which snap back onto her skin. I slide off the stage. I feel sick.

The music explodes in my ears. A thousand people are pushing toward the stage. I still see them as shadows. See Janosch fall off the stage, laughing like a lunatic. Troy's sitting in a corner with a glass of white beer, watching Angélique, who's in the act of throwing her panties into the audience. Fat Felix is in the same corner, and there's a plate of roast pork in front of him. He's grinning from ear to ear.

"What more could you want?" he asks. "Beautiful women and good food. I'm in paradise!" He sticks a forkful of pork into his mouth. Troy laughs.

"You guys know you're the best," I say. "The best I ever had."

"Yeah, yeah, we know," says Glob. "You're smashed."

"I may be, but you guys know you're the best, the best I ever had."

"Yeah, and you're the best we ever had too," says Glob crossly. "We know!"

"You're the best of the best," says Troy and starts laughing again.

"We're all the best," I say. "Heroes. *Crazy.*"

Janosch comes stumbling over to us. Sambraus is standing in the corner where there's a pay phone. His mouth is wide open. His eyes are empty and far away.

I know that I don't know a thing. I open my eyes. The back seat on which I am sitting is upholstered in brown leather. The back of the front seat has the Alfa Romeo logo on it. I can also see it on the steering wheel. It's black. Martin Lebert runs his hand

over it wearily. We're going through a crossroads.
Sambraus is sitting next to Lebert, pointing in various
directions. I'm sharing the back seat with the
guys. They're almost all asleep, except for Glob and
Skinny Felix, who have their faces pressed against
the window. It's pretty cramped in here. Troy and
Janosch are sitting one on top of the other, both
asleep. Janosch has his mouth wide open. Periodically
his tongue, which is bright red, flicks out. Florian
has propped himself up against his shoulder. I
yawn. My head hurts. Outside the sun is blazing. I
look at the time: 10:09.

"Where are we going?" I ask.

"To the cemetery," says Sambraus. "My friend
from school, Xavier Mils, is buried there. I found
out last night that he died." Sambraus swallows.

"And how did I get to be in this car?" I ask.

"Lebert carried you," he says. "We couldn't wake
you up. We managed with the others. You were the
only one we couldn't, so we had to lug you into the
car. And after we're done, we're going straight back
to Neuseelen."

"Straight back to Neuseelen?" I echo, appalled.

"Yes," says Sambraus. "We'll tell them we picked
you up."

"Picked us up where?" I ask, confused.

"You know, in the village," says Sambraus. "You
just came down on a lark or something. Lost track of

time. And after eleven p.m. nobody can get back into school, because the gates are locked."

"D'you think they'll believe us? And what about trying to phone?" I make my right hand into a receiver.

"Of course they'll believe you. There was simply no phone to be found or something."

"D'you think it'll work?"

"It'll work," says Lebert. "You just apologize for all the trouble you've caused, and that's that. It was only one night!"

So saying, he turns onto a side street.

I run my hands through my hair. My head aches. The thought of going back to Neuseelen makes me feel sick. I bend over to one side.

"You tied one on last night," says Lebert. He looks back at me. "You were really getting it on with Angélique. Which is why you lost out with Laura. But she was certainly doing her stuff. At least the others all got some!" He points to the guys.

"What are you thinking?" he asks.

"It's okay," I say. I'm lying. I clench my hands together.

Fat Felix turns to me. His eyes are glassy and his face is red. His hair is a mess.

"I'm sorry," he says, stretching his arms in front of him. "I have to ask you something again. I know I keep asking you things."

"Don't worry about it," I say. "People have to ask questions, otherwise they'd never understand anything. But I don't know if I can answer you. Sometimes it's the answers you don't understand."

"What was all that?" says Fat Felix. "Breaking out of school. Running away. The bus. The train. The subway. The strip joint. What was all that for? What was the point? How would you describe it? Life?"

I think. It's all a bit much for my shattered head. I take a deep breath. Open my mouth. "Maybe you could call it a story, one written by life."

I clench my teeth together. Sweat is running down my forehead. Glob goes round-eyed, and he rubs his hand across his face.

"Was it a good story? What was it about? Friendship? Having adventures?"

"It was about us. It was a boarding-school story— our boarding-school story."

"Is life full of stories?" asks Fat Felix.

"Lots," I say. "Happy stories, sad stories. And other stories. And all of them are different."

"Where do our boarding-school stories fit in?"

"Nowhere. None of the stories fits in any particular place. They lie around all over the place."

"Where?"

"On the path of life, as far as I know."

"That story with the girls four months ago, is that lying on the path of life too?"

"Yes."

"And where are we now?" he asks.

"We're on the path of life. Making and finding new stories."

Fat Felix leans his head against the window again. His eyes keep looking for something.

The cemetery is small. As is the grave. Almost nothing's been planted here. The gravestone is gray and rectangular. The writing on it is old. Looks like it dates from the last century. Xavier Mils must have been a very poor man. His initials are watched over by a Baby Jesus, who is looking up at us severely. Sambraus has squatted down by the grave and lays a bunch of white roses on it. Lebert stands beside him. We all stand back a little.

Janosch is the last to stumble up, muttering to himself, his hair every which way. He yawns and takes his position beside us.

"Old friend, I got here too late," says Sambraus, facing the gravestone. "I know. But I'm here now. I brought a few of the kids from the school with me. The new generation. You'd be proud of them! And my old friend Martin. You'd get on pretty well together, I think. He's really okay. . . ."

At this moment Fat Felix nudges me, and stares.

"Is this how all the stories end?"

"Yes, I think this is how they all end. But who knows? Maybe a whole new story is beginning. We don't decide that. All we can do is watch, wait, and see what's coming our way. And maybe that's the start of the new story."

Chapter 16

How can you describe life in boarding school? It's pretty difficult, I find. After all, it's just a life, like so many others on the planet. All I know is that you don't forget boarding school. Not for a second. Whether that's a good thing or not is for others to decide. For my part, all I can say is that you are forced into togetherness. Eternal togetherness. You live together, eat together, get into trouble. I speak from experience. You even have to cry together. Start crying when you're alone, and along comes someone right away who starts crying with you. I guess that's the way it has to be. Sometimes you wish you were dead. And sometimes you feel doubly alive. How can you describe life in boarding school? It goes by. I know that now.

The luggage is at the foot of the bed. Janosch has helped me pack. Three suitcases and a bag. Now they're all in a neat row. Ready to go. I swallow. It suddenly looks so empty in here. The walls are bare. Nothing on the desk anymore. A strange feeling goes through my body and I touch my right hand to my sweaty face. I got a 6 in math again. And a 5 in German. That's all it takes. I've been plowed again and have to leave the school. They wrote my parents a final letter that was really over the top: *Your son is unfortunately not capable of performing up to standard. In addition, he caused a great deal of trouble and was seen too often in the girls' corridor.*

My father will be here in ten minutes to collect me. That's how long I have to say goodbye to Janosch and the guys. They won't be leaving for summer vacation until tomorrow. Like everyone else. My father insisted on picking me up today, one day before the end of school. They let him. Apparently they can't get rid of me fast enough. I can't blame them. Fat Felix asks me what my father looks like. He puts his arm around my shoulder and I smile. My future looks quite bright. I'm to live with my father. He's moved out of the house altogether now and has rented a three-room apartment, on the edge of Schwabing in Milbertshofen. Apparently there are lots of young people there, according to him. Just right for me. I can't wait. I find myself thinking about Matthias Bochow. Then I'm supposed to go to some sort of special school. In Neuperlach. They don't put much emphasis on math there, according to my mother. But to tell the truth, I don't want to go. I'm sick of being the new boy all the time. The new boy carrying the letter.

Crazy

Thank God it's not a boarding school—I can go home in the afternoons. Cry. Laugh. Be happy. I'll soon be seventeen. People say life changes then, whether you like it or not. So probably mine will too. My physiotherapist says she sees a marked deterioration in my paralysis. My left hand keeps turning farther and farther inward. So does my left foot. She thinks at some point I'll no longer be able to walk. It's supposed to be a miracle I ever learned in the first place. But I'm still alive. And as long as that's true, it'll all go on somehow. At least that's what one of those philosophers said. Maybe it's true. Last time I had a weekend at home from school, I met this girl. Maybe that was a beginning. I don't know. She said she found me a little strange. When I told her lots of girls tell me that, she found it really strange. I don't know if it'll turn into something. If you want, you can visit me sometime. In Schwabing. After this whole thing you must know me pretty well. You'll find me quite easily. I'm the boy who drags his left leg in a weird way. I'm almost never in a crowd. And if I am, I'll be at the rear, at the back of the line. Apart from that, I'm to be found at a Rolling Stones concert with my father. Then I'm right at the front, next to the stage, because my father's always worried he won't get it all. But the Stones aren't going out on tour again anytime soon. Since the graduation dance at Neuseelen my hair has been bleach blond. I did it with the guys. We look really hilarious now.

Like brothers. Janosch thinks it's crazy. He's standing by the windowsill, propped on his elbows, swaying easily to and fro. Turns around. Knits his brows.

"Promise you'll take care of yourself?" he says.

"Look at me. Do I look as if I wouldn't take care of myself?"

Janosch laughs. He takes three steps toward me and gives me a hard hug.

"Come see us again, okay?" he says.

"Always." I pick up the overnight bag. Go over to the two Felixes. Hug them. "Take care, guys." The two Felixes look at me.

"Be well, old guy! Believe in yourself," says Glob. Skinny Felix nods and holds out his hand. I go over to Florian a.k.a. Girl. Embrace him.

"We had some good times together, huh," I say.

"Great times. Bye, Benni."

I go to Troy. He butts his head into my stomach.

"On your way," he says to me, and gives me his hand.

"Goodbye, Troy."

Anna and Malen are standing at the door. One after the other they throw their arms around my neck. They've painted goodbye cards for me which they stick into my bag. Marie didn't come. But she wasn't expected. Five minutes later my father appears. He comes in, moving quickly, collects the rest of the luggage, and is out of the room again immediately. I wave at the others and follow him.

Crazy

Turn around once more. Through the open door I see my friends. Raise my right hand. Then go along Tarts' Alley after my father. He holds open the door to the stairs for me. Richter, the headmaster, passes us there.

"Happy vacation," he mumbles to himself, marching on past us and into the Landorf corridor. We go down the stairs. It's a long flight. When we reach the bottom, I put down the bag. I'm exhausted.